In Paul Trout's world, happiness originates from two equal and potentially conflicting impulses: The need for privacy and the drive to play bass guitar at the highest possible volume. This is his story.

Paul Trout

Resonance

Paul Trout

Paul Trout

D:/resonance_book/front_matter

My first mistake: Saving this file. I didn't want anyone to ever read it, but didn't want to throw it away either. The mountain house where I'd spent my first 30 years was under new management, and everything within its rustic walls was endangered.

I wasn't willing to move the bulky computer cross country to my new San Francisco home, so I copied the file to a floppy. There were three in my suitcase, two in plain black and a third with a bright "PC Eye," my employer's logo. I chose color, but life would be different now if I'd stuck with black.

My second mistake: Taking the disk to work, thinking that I was going to print it out some night for posterity. Instead I put it in a drawer, where it sat for nearly two years. Where it was discovered and examined by the the magazine's new owners. My little diary caught the attention of the CEO, who informed me by memo that he wanted to publish it to inaugurate a new line of prestige books that had nothing to do with computers. Tech was all good enough, but everyone had to prepare for when it crashed and burned. I wondered what that would look like, because I was never going to touch a typewriter again. Certainly not to write a second book.

The CEO, Willem Wagner, bought the magazine and book divisions from the proceeds of the sale of his company to IBM. The market leader was selling a new line of computers, the PS/2, and was now offering a network project manager as an option.

I'd met Wagner before, when he had unsuccessfully demoed his version 1.0 at our office and gotten pissed because a colleague had failed to pronounce his name as "Villem." In retaliation, I had written a perfunctory review. So I anticipated some ill feeling. Imagining that his first words would be "bet you wish you'd accepted my invitation to see the demo in our own office. Because right now, I own you."

Instead he was respectful and deferential. Sort of. These were warm sentiments, but his eyes were still icy and distrusting. He dropped the happy stuff when we started talking about my future. Pete, my mentor, was gone, and the magazine was moving its main editorial offices to Boston. There would still be a San Francisco bureau, which I would lead. I was no longer required to cover the news, rather I would concentrate on columns, long features and developing myself into an expert who would be quoted on television and speak at trade shows.

What I never wanted. But I nodded, knowing I needed to stifle the urge to just get up and leave, or just push back. Knowing that I would do so, soon enough.

He wanted to publish my book, titled *Resonance*, describing it as a "new wave memoir." This was the kind of book, he said, that would become very popular, modern recollections told from an unreliable narrator's point of view.

"I don't believe half of the stuff you say in here," he said. "But you probably are convinced that most of this happened."

My "soon enough" challenge came sooner than expected.

"I never meant for this to be published," I said. "Like you pointed out, it's not exactly factual and it's more than a little embarrassing. I do not want to be associated with this."

He said that he really didn't need my permission, since it qualified as 'work product." It was on a company-labeled disk inside a company-owned desk, so it belonged to the company.

"What if I just quit?" I asked.

"I'll publish it anyway," he said. "We need to build our new catalog, even if the stuff isn't that good at first." Hold the flattery. "But I need you to edit this and agree to promote it, if you want to keep that book contract you just signed with your mother. I know you really want to write that one."

That was unexpected. Denise and I were just starting to connect. I didn't want to lose that.

Wagner's plan was for me to work on the book full time . When I finished I could take a few months off and come back in the spring to open and lead the West Coast Bureau. The job offer was a pretty cool opportunity. Selling out doesn't always have to be a bad thing. So I told him fine.

He still didn't really trust me, as each of my changes to the manuscript needs to be justified in a linked note. This pissed me off, because it meant I could not sabotage or scuttle the project. He may be manipulative but he's not stupid.

I still managed to decrease the disaster potential. I smoothed out the language and editing out all the really embarrassing and personal stuff. I took out all the sex, which wasn't anybody's business anyway. We don't need to hear another story about a 13-year-old kid losing their virginity to a cheerleader in the eleventh grade, or sleeping with their father's girlfriends. In the notes, I said these people would sue us for slander. The word "lawsuit" is like Kryptonite to an amateur publisher, so I didn't have to justify these cuts any further.

There is always a flaw in the system. Here, each change to the manuscript required an explanatory note, but the program allowed me to paste in material at the beginning and the end of the book in separate folders without approval. That was, as long as I don't change the "Front Matter" placeholder file name. It cheapens the project but that's OK with me if it looks cheesy.

Here's the truth: This book is being published against my will. If you are reading this, you are invading my privacy. It's as if I came over to your house, stole an old diary and published it for everyone to see. There is nothing in here of any interest to anyone. You should just put this down and move on.

On top of that, Villain Vagner is a manipulating asshole and he can shove his book deal. Denise has her own friends in publishing and we signed a new contract.

So yeah, Villie, I quit. Do your worst. I'm not coming back.

Paul Trout
November 1, 1987

November 1, 1984

I taped over the cricket's bright red eyes but can't get away from that insipid artificial grin.

It's day four of the great technical support experiment. The phone has yet to ring. I'm sitting here staring at the screen doing nothing at all or reading inconsequential magazines and newspapers. It's all about the election, which is itself inconsequential. Everyone hates Reagan, but he's going to win again.

So instead of staring at a blinking cursor waiting for the phone I decided to see what this little machine can do. I loaded up something called Wordstar and began writing it all down. I'll tell my story until the phone rings.

My name is Paul Trout, but I am known to most people around here as Hamster. My name changed when I was twelve, when Artie Connors and I were hiking through the woods and met David Steel and his pals. Steel, the very model of a modern major bully, was wandering around the forest looking for animals to torture. Instead he found us.

I was about five feet tall at the time, and round. This appearance was helped along by my coat, a big brown thing that made me look like a blimp. I was wearing a fur hat with long black earmuffs that usually tied below my chin but were flapping around because I didn't need the extra warmth.

My cheeks and nose were bright red, with a trail of snot dribbled on my face.

Steel, a year older and a foot taller, was dressed in a shiny black leather jacket that went halfway down his thigh and a wool cap that covered his arrogant head stubble.

"Look at the little hamster," he sneered, pushing me. I wobbled but didn't fall down. "Someone left their stupid pet in the rain."

Steel had pushed me around before. I knew that a wisecrack response wasn't productive. He would do whatever he wanted. The only strategy was to wait until he lost interest. If the past was any indication that would occur in about four minutes.

"He needs a new name," Steel snarled. "How about 'Ham-hole? That fits him better than his coat and hat."

He pushed me again, and I fell on my ass with my hands in the snow and legs extended.

"Hamster-hole," he went on.

"You can't come up with anything better than that?" Artie's voice was quivering. Shut up Artie. You should know better. I got up and dusted myself off. Which might have been a mistake, because Steel would probably knock me down again.

"Like what, grandma boy?" Artie was about my size and had no more ability to challenge Steel than I did, but would regularly kick Steel's ass in English class with his articulations. Steel would mangle the language in class and Artie would jump up and correct him. It was the opposite in math class. Steel was an astonishing numbers prodigy who could figure out algebraic equations in his head. He could probably do calculus pretty well, but he sneered at his own ability as if he were ashamed.

"Don't you mean grammar boy?" Artie said, his voice stronger.

"Hamster hole," Steel said again. "I'm gonna put you two in a cage and throw it off a cliff."

"It would be really heavy because they are both really fat," a crony named Billy said, his own voice wavering. I realized that Billy was as scared of Steel as we were. He needed to say something and was hoping that it was funny.

Steel laughed. Billy relaxed.

We were all quiet for a while when Steel spoke quietly.

"Little Paulie here is just a little Hamster-fuck."

I was astonished that Steel knew my first name while hoping he did not remember my surname. In that case there'd be an extended round of smelly fish jokes. Also disturbing was how four minutes had passed and he was still here.

Steel's laugh was interrupted by three loud gunshots, in close range.

"Let's go," he said, pushing me hard. I rolled down the hill. They started running toward the gunshots. I was already halfway down the hill and continued down the hill. Artie tagged behind me.

"What kind of idiot runs toward gunshots?" I asked Artie. I thought that it would be a good thing if he got shot and missed school for a few days.

I blamed myself, then, when Steel didn't show up for school the next day, or the next. After two weeks I was starting to relax. Billy wandered around the school looking lost, like a nervous rat who lost his master. Two can play this rodent game. We soon heard that Steel had moved away, that his parents had kicked him out. It was possible he had some real problems. I began to feel sympathy, recalling how some kids that are bullied one year become friends with their tormentors the next.

I hoped that "Hamster" had disappeared along with Steel and was still a little paranoid, to the point of hearing something that sounded like "Hey-Hamster" when I was walking through the halls. It got louder and more frequent, until it was accompanied by eye contact and lip movement. After someone said "throw Hamster the ball" in gym class I knew it was here to stay.

How did this happen? I was going to ask Billy about it but every time I looked at him he scurried away. Steel's other cronies weren't close enough to hear the conversation, or bright enough to remember what was said.

I figured it out. On the first day of Spring I turned to whom I thought was my best friend and said "Artie. What the fuck?"

Over the summer we'd zigzag up the mountain, which was littered with abandoned artists' cabins. If the window or the door were unlocked we'd go right in and make ourselves at home. Turns out they might not have been abandoned after all. We'd go through their stuff but would never steal anything, which made it OK. That was the rule, one time we brought another guy, Bruce, on our little hike. We slipped into a little house, one we'd been in before, he took a jackknife from a table and put it in his pocket.He glared at us, daring us to do something. We didn't, aside from not inviting him along again.

We didn't break into every house but did lots of snooping. We'd look at the house from far away, hiding in the woods to see whether anyone was living there. With no sign of life we might move a bit closer, look into the window and make up a story about what's inside. If someone was moving around we would make up another kind of story, like the guy who had no shirt on a cold afternoon. His little multi-building lot was really a nudist colony, he heard us coming and didn't have time to put on all his clothes. He moved around as if he didn't know we were there, but we both knew otherwise. There was a creepy air, everywhere.

One old lady lived in a house surrounded by goats, so we went for the obvious, christening her as "The Goat Lady." We'd get on top of a hill with binoculars and watch her for a while. She had long, white hair, a billowing garment, and a craggy face.

We wrote her whole history in our heads, casting her as a witch who controlled the goats through spells. It was obvious to us that the Goat Lady was capturing kids and turning them into goats. We looked at each other and had the same thought as we heard something move.

A goat was heading toward us from the meadow below. When it got closer we saw that it had one eye and a single antler along with a marking that looked like an S on its face. It was snarling at us. It charged into the brush and started kicking us, but the attack stopped after a loud whistle. Right then, the Goat Lady stood up in her garden, looked straight at where we were hiding and waved for us to come down.

"Did you see that goat's face, the S over his eye?" Artie whispered. "The goat is fucking Steel, reborn."

We walked down the hill, expecting her to start yelling, or worse, call our parents and complain about our trespassing that had happened before. Instead she smiled, invited us to sit down at a picnic table and poured us some lemonade.

She told us her name, Mrs. Babian, adding that "many people just call me the goat lady, and I don't mind that." Obviously she could read minds. She had most of her teeth, but there were several hairs coming out of her chin and cheek that she didn't seem to know about. She couldn't possibly, as they were so weird that no one in their right mind would go out in public like that.

Or maybe sitting outside her own house on her own land she really wasn't in public.

Paul Trout

She asked us what brought us up this trail, and what we knew of the town's history. We said we did, a little, and started squirming, figuring out a way to get out of there. It was too far in the woods to say we heard our parents calling. We looked at our watches and saw we didn't need to be home for another two hours. Lying wasn't an option as Mrs. Babian had already proven she could see through us.

We began to fidget, but everything changed when she began to talk. She was 73 years old and had lived in here since her mid 30s and remembered how it was before anything got developed. She talked slowly and clearly. We got sucked in right away.

Everyone thinks their home town is unique and special. But Wheeler's Blue Notch really is.

When you approach the mountains from either direction, west or east, there are the expected hills and bounces and a wide, flat space about a third of the way down. That's where our town is.

There are breaks in the mountains, fifty miles north and eighty miles south of the big notch, so a cross-country drive means that it will be either on the left or the right. There are cutoff roads that take you to closer, although from the east it is a smooth four lanes while the western path is a rough route that alternates between pavement and dirt.

The easier eastern access resulted from more development at the foothills. Which isn't necessarily a bad thing, although what happened on the ground had some negative effects on those of living in the sky.

Early settlers saw the mountains from a distance and the north and south passes, so it didn't occur to them to go up the middle. Someone eventually did, maybe to avoid the crowd, crawling up a four-mile trail to end up on a plateau that measured ten miles wide and from one to three miles deep. There was nothing up there aside from an astonishing view, to the east or the west. The land was good enough to grow some vegetables, but there was ready protein available from the earth (deer) and the sky (birds).

The original crew, arriving around 1880, wasn't seeking gold or new opportunity, just a gentle, quiet place where they could live their lives and create.

They were all artists, so they were surprised by the harsh weather and what it took to survive. Fortunately, some of their kids rebelled and learned how to build houses and roads.

The notch looked razor-straight from a distance. Up close there were crooks and nannies where people built shacks and artist sheds built inside the small canyons. They built a small downtown area, dubbed Notch Boulevard, with the necessary stores and businesses. Old photos look like the TV depictions of western towns I watched when I was growing up. Instead of cowboys and fancy ladies there were men in dresses and pointy beards and women with short hair and sharp teeth.

But Mrs. Babian knew many of the historical details, aside from what we had heard or made up. She told us how the settlers, seeing the layout of the land, chose north or south for their western journey.

Except a guy named Silas Wheeler, a spoiled New York City rich kid who settled at the bottom of the hill. He claimed the surrounding land and began ranching, not before establishing a "town" at the foothills and naming it after himself. He brought in dozens of his spoiled friends who were itching for a Western adventure. They were surprised when they arrived in Wheeler and were expected to herd cattle. Most of them had nowhere else to go so they played along and, surprisingly, began earning a good living. The rest of them crawled up the four-mile trail to the plateau and joined the already thriving artist colony.

Twenty years on Wheeler—the man and the town—was thriving, and the artist colony had grown to a few hundred people. The artists depended on Wheeler for food and supplies, while Wheeler's citizens were eager to place the artists' painting and sculpture into their new homes.

Wheeler, the man, built a 300-room four story hotel and ballroom, modeled after the posh resorts that dotted New York's Hudson River Valley. He called it the Wheeler Mountain House. Guests trickled in for the first few years until one of the visitors, a writer, published a piece in a New York newspaper about the magical west. It was not all stagecoaches and dust, the article stated, there was culture in those plains and mountains. Not very many people came from New York for a vacation, but many travelers on a westward journey would stop in for a week or two, even if it took them 100 miles out of their way.

They all asked the same question, whether there was a more direct route to the other side of the mountain. Sick of saying the same thing repeatedly, Wheeler printed up a leaflet. Yes, it was possible to cut through instead of going around, but required a four-mile trip up a pockmarked dirt road. The views from the top were astonishing, but not really worth the trip (to demonstrate he attached a grainy photograph of the landscape). Once on the plateau travelers would need to practically crawl down the other side, on trails that were barely visible but you couldn't get lost as long as you headed straight down. Mrs. Babian had one of these flyers.

She knew that I lived in the Blue Notch Mountain House. She asked whether I was aware of its history. I said that I knew some of it.

In the early 1920s Arnold Wheeler came to town. He was Silas Wheeler's spoiled rich grand nephew who had just graduated law school. After "an indiscretion with a young woman," as Mrs. Babian put it, Arnold was dispatched westward to act as the town's first attorney. He got richer, brokering and muddying land deals while running a gambling room in the back of his office.

Unlike many Wheeler residents Arnold traveled for months at a time, seeing the sights and exploring different cultures. On one trip to Amarillo he stopped at a restaurant and ordered a chicken fried steak. He liked chicken and steak; so this was bound to taste great.

There was no chicken involved, as the recipe coats a small slab of poor quality beef with a layer of batter normally used for fried chicken. On his return to Wheeler Arnold approached his uncle with a request to serve the newly discovered delicacy in the hotel's restaurant. He even brought back an extra order in a wooden box for Silas to taste. Except when he opened the box the food was half-eaten by rats.

Silas was not convinced. He was getting sick of Arnold's whining. Silas told Arnold that the Wheeler Mountain House would serve chicken fried steak "over his dead body," instantly regretting the comparison. Arnold was approaching this idea with homicidal fervor.

Silas would often contradict Arnold just for sport, but this was a matter of principal and taste. He looked down on hamburgers and fried chicken as food for the poor and uncultured. Combining them was like crossbreeding a cat and a cockroach. He was about to use the argument that the recipe was a waste of good meat before realizing that the beef contained was often of the worst quality.

Still, Arnold persisted. He'd come in every day for lunch, pondering over the menu for a while, and then ordering chicken fried steak. When he was told that it was not available he would stand up angrily and leave, not paying for his coffee.

The waitresses were generally tolerant and participated in the charade, but a few refused to go through the motions. Hazel Earnshaw, then a mature fourteen years old, would cry every time she waited on Arnold. Silas, who fancied Hazel but was too proper to make a move, noticed her discomfort and came up with a plan.

The next day Arnold came in and began the little word play. When he placed his order Hazel didn't start crying but said "wait a minute, sir" and left the room. Silas returned moments later, sitting down and looking Arnold directly in the eye.

"If you want a chicken fried steak you should open your own fucking hotel."

Arnold became very still. A few moments later Arnold left quietly, leaving a dollar coin on the table. Quite a tip for a five cent tab. Silas split it with Hazel, 70 percent to 30 percent.

Arnold never came in again. Silas didn't miss the business, since there wasn't much, and surely didn't miss the aggravation. Arnold abandoned his law practice and was rarely seen in town. In the spring Arnold came into Silas' hotel and paid for 20 rooms in advance, putting five people in each room. This crew of 100 began building a road up the mountain, using the dirt path as a guide but using switchbacks to ease the ascent. During construction, people noticed a small rectangular rise in the center of the notch, which grew taller as the months went on.

Arnold had taken the dare. He was building his own hotel.

"Do you name your goats?" Artie asked Mrs. Babian.
"I do," she said.
"What's that one over there?" Artie asked, pointing to the S-branded creature who was still snarling at us.
"That's David," she said. "He showed up in the spring out of nowhere. I asked him his name and he said "Daaaaaaaave."
`"We gotta go," Artie said.

November 2

Today I left my rooms, had breakfast at the café, and walked to the office that we turned into a computer room. There was a piece of brown construction paper taped to the door with "SMUG must die" stenciled on. I ripped it down, tore it up, and put it in the trash. It was ridiculous, anyway. The old band was not getting back together. The Beatles—with one dead member—were more likely to reunite than SMUG, at this point.

I need to put this in context, why I'm not exactly chuffed about Artie's little assignment. It's true that I'm not doing much else, but that's the point. I really don't have the same accomplishment drive as people my age. Or any other age.

Most people, when they graduate high school, want to go out and see the world. Make a contribution. Make a change. They realize soon enough their relative existence and strive toward their own happiness. When they get a realistic idea of how much they can do for the world they come home to where they started and build a contented life.

I wanted to short cut that. I'll skip college, hitching around the world, getting a job in the big city, getting married, having kids only to be defeated by life and return home.

So I never left. And I don't need to hear about far off places like Israel or Alabama I could visit to gain enrichment. It's not that I'm lazy, or completely unmotivated. I need to work, stay busy, but helping to run a hotel is a path to a varied life. I own the place so I can do as much or as little as I want, and implement my own ideas without having to run them through a boss or a board of directors.

Aside from my so-called job I like it up here. The air is clean, the view is great, and I can have anything that I really need delivered. If it's something that remotely connects to the hotel I can get it as part of the business.

As for the more frivolous things; books, music, clothes, I can call ahead for them in Wheeler and have someone bring it up to me the next day.

Wheeler is getting too crowded, too crazy. So you don't want to hear what I have to say about big places like Albuquerque or Lubbock. I went to Washington DC once for about a week and almost lost my mind for all the people. All the energy and information flowing in simultaneously like a firehose. You have to jump aside, or it will knock you over.

You walk into a newsstand and see papers from New York, San Francisco, and Dallas to start. Do you have the time to read all of them? If you don't do you feel left out or uninformed? And the magazines. News from all sizes, and news about celebrities. I get lost reading *People*, then realize I haven't read *Us*. The *Enquirer* and the *Star* provide more depth, detail, and viewpoints. Where does it end? Do I really need to know everything.

So by staying out of the way, living in a town where there are no fancy-ass out of town newsstands protects me from this deluge of unwelcome information. I've seen people who can't go to lunch without a magazine or take a shit without a newspaper. The human brain is only so large, but we are told we need to stuff it full until it bursts.

Not my brain. I don't want to change the world. Some days I don't even want to change my socks.

Artie and I hiked up to see Mrs. Babian again. We were about to knock on the door when she threw it open. She looked as if she had just gotten up, so we immediately thought that we should have called first.

"Oh, Paul," she said. "Arthur." I broke my glasses and didn't recognize you right away. You want to come in, or sit on the porch?"

It was a little chilly so we chose inside. Artie picked up her broken glasses without asking, sat down and pulled out a little toolkit. After about 45 seconds he handed them to her, repaired.

"Thank you Arthur," she said. "Do you boys want tea, coffee, lemonade, or vodka?" We chose tea, and she picked up where she'd left off before.

There was something familiar about the inside of the house. I'd smelled this combination of wood, textiles and overcooked food before. I got used to it after a few minutes, when it became oddly comforting.

I knew the rest of the story, since it was my own.

Arnold opened his mountaintop hotel, visible for miles on both sides of the mountain range, in 1926. It wasn't as large as the Wheeler Mountain House with just 60 rooms, but it was as glorious. Giant featherbeds. A sparkling ballroom adjoining a fancy restaurant. And a café that was nearly as large as the restaurant, serving gritty, tasty, "working class" food. Which included chicken fried steak and hamburgers.

He hired Hazel who now had around 10 years of food experience, to run the place. She quit her job with Sila' and took some rooms at the hotel. The same rooms she occupied years later when I knew her, as my grandmother.

Since the new hotel was actually on the mountain. Since Arnold's last name was Wheeler it was christened as "The Real Wheeler Mountain House: On a Real Mountain." Arnold was still pissed at Silas, apparently. No one else cared about the feud since the story had been told a million times. Arnold sensed this, opting for the simpler "Blue Notch Mountain House."

Like the original Wheeler Mountain House, the new place was priced beyond the means of the locals. Silas didn't care since he had plenty of traffic from the outside world. The townsfolk also lacked class, so Silas allowed as few of them inside as possible.

Blue Notch was farther out of the way, though cars could now drive up the zig zag road to the summit.

Arnold had also bought the land next to Silas' place which he used to locate the bottom stop of a cable car that shot right up the mountain. It never really opened for business because they couldn't get it to work reliably and correctly. But the sign "This is the path to the Blue Notch Mountain House" is still there today.

The Notch, as it was soon nicknamed, never got the chance to flourish. It was higher and colder than the place at the foot of the hill, with the added disadvantage of a shaky electrical system. Arnold had put a powerful wood stove in each room, but the guests were less enamored of wood heat than the innkeeper.

Arnold didn't know how to run a hotel, so it was lacking in finesse. His one wise decision was to finance the hotel himself, without involving any banks. This ended up as good news in the long run. When the stock market crashed no one could take it away from him. Less so in the short run as he had used all his money to build the place with not enough left to operate it properly.

The only exception was the Blue Notch Café, which Hazel had turned into big business, relatively. This was a brilliant move, as locals who could not afford to dine in the restaurant, sleep in the suites or rent the ballroom for a wedding flocked to the place all day and all of the night. Which translated to 7 a.m. to 11 p.m.

The even kept the hotel afloat after the 1929 stock market crash. Arnold could have at least kept the hotel open should anyone have the $20 discount rate. But it was too much work, and he'd grown bored. Using the crash as an excuse he said he was going to New York City to work in Wheeler's, a family owned department store in lower Manhattan. Prior to this, the few people who heard Arnold talk about his New York family got the feeling he didn't like them very much. He became the absent manager, returning once or twice a year to inspect the property.

On his last trip, around the end of 1935, he deeded the entire Blue Notch Inn—the hotel, restaurant, , land and the cable car— to my grandmother with no strings attached. Other than she would need to keep the place going and pay the property taxes. This wasn't much of a change for Hazel who had been running things for a while.

Hazel was glad Arnold was out of the picture. He continually took on new projects he couldn't handle, made commitments he could not honor and took too much food at the hotel buffet. Hazel was the opposite. She carved out a wing for herself and her staff, closing down 60 rooms and the restaurant. This stayed pretty much the same until she died in 1966, although there was a rotating cleaning crew that kept things from getting too musty.

Right before Arnold left Hazel married Jack Trout, the restaurant's gourmet chef. Pretty soon people who ate at the restaurant only on special occasions came in a few times a week. It was the same food at one fourth the price.

Hazel channelled her efforts into the café. That, and raising her infant son, Walter. My father.

Sometime in the 1930's the town was incorporated as "Wheeler's Blue Notch" but ended up on the map as "Wheeler's Notch." People living "in the Notch" had to go down the hill to shop for anything other than the essentials. The Notch had its own elementary school, but after sixth grade I made the trip up and down every day.

The phone rang in the middle of my last sentence.

"Cricket Computer user support. This is Paul. How can I help you?"

"Paolo. Que Pasa?" Artie was one of the few people who didn't call me Hamster. He never called me Paul either, it was always something like Paulo, Pablo, Pavel, Paul-boy or Pauley-wanna-cracker.

"No one's called yet," I said.

"They wouldn't have," he said. "It'll be a few days. We are having a little delay getting them ramped up for delivery. The packaging isn't perfect."

The packaging sucked to begin with. The computer didn't look anything like the competition. Instead of an off-white or beige color they were pale green. Instead of a separate computer, monitor and keyboard the monitor slid into a groove on top of the computer and the keyboard extended from an attached drawer. Both the computer and the monitor had small plastic molded crickets on the front, with the eyes lighting up red when the power was on. It was creepy.

The really stupid part: At startup, instead of an innocuous beep it emitted a strangled chirp.

Artie asked what I thought.

"Most people don't like this shade of green," I said. "It looks like frog's blood. Even if they like green they surely hate bugs. You might as well call it the cockroach. And that chirp is annoying."

"They'll get used to it," he said. "When you compare it to the competition this is a really cool design. As for the chirp, people need to learn to leave the computer on all the time and not turn it off at night like a TV. If they hate the chirp enough it will motivate them to follow the instructions."

My best-ever friend wasn't very good at listening to other people or notions that his grand ideas missed the mark. I knew he would ignore my feedback, that asking what I thought was reflexive to him and his mind was already swirling around the next idea. That didn't stop me from speaking up, just once. Not that ever saying "I told you so" would have made an impression.

"Something else," I said. "I got this weird note today, a piece of brown paper with 'SMUG must die' on it. I don't get the point here, since SMUG is as dead as Jesus. I hope no one thinks we're going to do this again."

"Yeah, I got one too," he said. "I'll bet that Randy and Sparky got them, but I doubt they got through to Lois with the security and all."

He took a breath.

"Sooo," he drew it out. "I'm guessing that you haven't picked up your bass or given any thought to what I told you about this opportunity for the band."

"I thought you were joking," I said. "What I heard was about the computer project. I thought you gave me the bass because you thought it was something I wanted, and that I was sorry for selling my old one."

"You never listen to me, man," he said. "We've got to talk about that sometime."

Mrs. Babian was in her kitchen, with the afternoon light turning the smoke from her cigarette into a multicolored mist. It swirled around her and she stared into space for a moment.

"You are the one they call Hamster," she said after a while. "It fits you."

That statement didn't require a response.

She picked up her story about the town and the family history. I had grown up with the generalities, outline of the family history. How Jack had joined the army just before World War II as a cook. He served, literally, until the end of the war. He survived the battles but never returned to his wife and son.

The Blue Notch continued to thrive and became the only decent restaurant option in town. When Prohibition ended Hazel turned what was once the hotel gift shop into a liquor store and began serving spirits at the café, over the counter. She renovated the old restaurant and offered it cheap to Mark Connors, Artie's grandfather, so he could relocate his general store. She planned to clear out the

ground floor rooms and turn them into small shops, but
that fizzled when the war started.

I heard all this before and was starting to doze a bit.
Mrs. Babian chose that moment to deliver some real
news.

"Mr. Trout, Your life is somewhat more interesting
than you imagine," she said adding that Jack Trout did not
die in the war, as I thought. He survived, but did not
return out of disloyalty or sloth. Rather, he had met
another soldier, Arnold Wheeler Jr. Mr. Wheeler was
aware of Blue Notch and the hotel because his father had
brought him there when he was very young.

Arnold Junior was raised in New York but only saw
his father sporadically until the depression. Jack figured
out that Arnold Senior always had a family in New York,
which he never mentioned while he was in Blue Notch.
His defection to New York was not because he couldn't
handle the stress of the hotel business but because his
wife had given him an ultimatum. Return to New York
now, she said, or never come back again. I will raise our
son alone, and you can be in charge of the other one when
it arrives.

Jack figured out that the "other one" was Walter. He
remembered how Hazel, after showing little interest in
him for years, suddenly seduced him one night after his
shift. The relationship continued and was, in Jack's mind,
pretty rewarding. A few months later when she
announced her pregnancy Jack said he would marry her
right away. Arnold senior performed the ceremony, and
Jack settled into life as the hotel's assistant manager.

Jack discovered that Walter was not his child and
Hazel had lied to him for years. In battle Jack began to
think of Hazel as an evil harridan who was worse than the
Germans. In Jack's eyes, Walter evolved from a creative,
curious child into an ever-enlarging ball of flesh.

Hazel had told the lie so many times she had
forgotten what the truth was. She was surprised by Jack's

angry letter. The war has turned him into a bitter man, she thought, and I don't want that kind of bitterness in my home. She told Walter that Jack had died in battle. Walter felt sadness, but looked on the bright side. His father was a hero who died saving the country. This made him special, as he had noble blood.

Walter, however, was a talented dilettante with an inability to commit to anything long enough to make it work. As far as I know, he still doesn't know the truth.

"You are entitled to a great deal more than you have," Mrs. Babian said. "When I last visited, the big city Wheeler's New York was crowded and successful. That legacy belongs to you."

Whatever this money was it wasn't really mine, I thought at the time. Today, I recognize this discomfort because it was certain to make me lazy. Just like Walter, Artie and Arnold, all who ended up with money they didn't deserve.

November 3

That Artie admitted that "we don't listen to each other" was his first-ever acknowledgement that he didn't listen to me.

Two weeks ago he arrived and pulled a cart full of boxes into the lobby, where I was sweeping the floor. He barged in here and disrupted my life. In the space of 90 minutes, he convinced me to drop everything I was doing to join a venture that is guaranteed to fail. He also got me to agree to a band reunion. It's not that I'm a complete pushover, he challenged my every misgiving with a reasonable option and there was no way to say no. Aside from that, I don't have any pressing obligations. Saying no, in the end, would be a lot more difficult than the alternative.

"Paul-boy," he announced. "We will need a room."

We began talking, about his new idea and where I fit in.

Six months ago he was hanging around the state capitol when he was approached by a kid named Delbert asking whether he wanted a good deal on a computer. Delbert was tall with a wispy beard and an undefinable odor. Just like your average drug dealer. Artie listened to the pitch and found that Delbert had spent his college years dealing computers first by purchasing overstocked IBM PCs. These machines were at a premium and were not affordable to the business itself, so he took one apart and built his own to the same specifications. Reverse engineering, he called it.

The standard IBM PC market shrank, as the company released the newer, more expensive, and harder to reverse engineer PC-AT. Delbert began building his own design on a larger scale, and was selling them through limited channels. He supported the operation by selling cheap Mexican weed, and hadn't been able to differentiate his sales pitch.

Artie, sitting in a bar wearing his trademark polka-dot bow tie along with stovetop striped jeans and a pair of fucking Hushpuppies, a polka dot bow tie looked like an easy mark, if not for computers then an ounce or two of weed.

Delbert was actually the mark, although he didn't know it yet.

Restless Artie had built a concert promotion business with SMUG as the first client, building it into the largest in the state. He sold it to the famous promoter Bill Graham who was seeking his own regional presence. Artie figured that Graham would open a competing agency anyway, so he cut his winnings.

He then opened a frozen yogurt stand in the capital, soon expanding to 30 stores. The plain-tasting yogurt was augmented by imaginative toppings like pecan fudge and banana puree. He had just sold these off when he met Delbert, and was seeking new opportunities.

Maybe he did deserve all that money.

Drawing on a paper placemat he sketched out a computer design that looked nothing like what Delbert and everyone else were selling. All the computers were about the same height and width, to accommodate standard-sized motherboards and expansion slots. Artie's sketch was two inches higher, as it added a keyboard drawer. Unlike the standard beige or brown it was a pale green, like a squashed caterpillar.

The monitor slid into a groove on the top of the central unit. He drew a bug on the top of the monitor with glowing eyes.

There would be an electrical connection between the computer and the monitor, he explained. When the power was turned on computer would make a grasshopper sound and the eyes would glow.

"But wait," Artie said. "There's more."

The front panel above the keyboard flipped up and was held in place by a folding metal arm. The computer's insides slid out on a second drawer, making it quick and easy to work on the innards.

Delbert was skeptical about everything else, but thought this part was really cool.

"I've been thinking about this for a while," Artie said. "Maybe you can tell."

They ordered another round and Artie began picking up the tab.

"I've been playing with the IBM PC and the Apple machines since the beginning," he said. "The new Apple Macintosh is clunky and weird but makes it clear that it needs to be graphically sophisticated. We start with high resolution monochrome and add color for the Grasshopper 2."

"I don't know man," Delbert said. "I like the drawer and the graphics but I'm not sure about the whole grasshopper thing. I don't know anyone who likes those little fuckers. And they are always jumping around in random patterns, the last thing you want a computer to do."

It was important, Delbert said, that people trusted their computers to not jump up the walls and start making weird noises.

"Alrighty then," Artie said. "We can call it the cricket. People like crickets."

Artie Connors, not listening to people since 1956.

Delbert was dazzled. He was so pumped about working for an actual computer company and becoming an industry player that he didn't bother to point out that crickets are as jumpy as grasshoppers.

"I've been playing with these things for a while, like I said," Artie said. "People in business aren't quite convinced using them is any better than a pad and paper, but they don't want to be left behind. Computer companies are looking to make as many units as possible so they can cash in before the granola chompers push them back to simplicity.

"We need to start small," Artie said, moving the familiarity line to mid field. "We build the computers to order. We sell them one at a time to people. We emphasize the fun part, instead of making it easier to fill out forms or prepare financial reports.

They did a handshake deal. Delbert would work on a new design and look around for technicians. Artie would manage the money, doling it out as needed to build the company. Artie would also finance a new location.

Two days later Artie walked into the dilapidated lobby of the Wheeler Mountain House, which was now a disco unsuccessfully operated by a woman who called herself Sunshine Peyote Wheeler. The old man's granddaughter, probably. He brought out a bag with $50,000 cash and a sales agreement. The agreement covered past taxes and ancillary cost, so Sunshine could just beam out of the building right now with more money than she ever imagined.

She didn't even bother to tell anyone about the sale, so the staff was puzzled upon arriving for their shift and finding a locked door. Artie was walking the floor inside but they couldn't get his attention. What a surprise.

Artie unpacked two Crickets and set them up. Delbert was outside playing with the phone box. They had installed a dedicated wire that connected a four line phone that was placed between the two computers. It had a speaker and a headset. He unpacked a large looseleaf notebook that described the Cricket inside and out, with subjects broken down by tabs. Each section had a list of expected questions and their descriptive answers.

"It's all spelled out, and you can read from the page if you want," he said. "But you may want to practice a few times so you can fake spontenaity."

After everything was in place he deigned to explain the process. Calls would come into the newly-renovated Cricket Mountain House and Manufacturing Facility in Wheeler. The technical questions would be routed to an engineer who would then take a break from the assembly line. The simpler user-based calls would be routed to me. "I'm having you do this because you have a great voice and a phone personality," he said. I never know when he's joking.

"It'll take a while for the calls to trickle in but I want to be ready when that happens," Artie said. "So you should get started on November 1."

I didn't have much to do in the wintertime as the hotel business slowed a bit and I wasn't really needed. Artie always assumed this was the case, that I would be eager to support any of his new ideas, out of the goodness of my heart.

"I need you to be doing this for three months," he said. "By that time we will either expand or go broke. I'll pay $2,000 a month, which I'll deposit to your bank account on the first of the month. The November payment is already there.

"I know that I've asked you to do a lot throughout the years and I don't expect you to do this out of the goodness of your heart," he said, showing some perception and self awareness. I knew it would pass and didn't have to wait long.

"One more thing," he said. "You may have some extra time in the beginning, so I thought you'd want to brush up on your bass playing."

I sold the beat-up Gibson EB-O ten years ago and never looked back. I never had any particular talent for the bass and hated being in a band. My playing was a happy diversion, but when I was alone I froze in front of people. After SMUG ended badly I had no desire to play or practice.

It's a beautiful instrument. A brand-new blue Gibson EB-O with metal flake sparkles. I'd never seen one of these. They kept it simple, with one pickup and three knobs. I couldn't keep my hands off the sculptured body. I didn't want to play, just to feel it for a while. I hadn't noticed Delbert who had unobtrusively wheeled in a small Marshall.

"We gotta go," Artie said. Delbert, silent throughout, began cleaning up. "See if you can't practice some of the old songs, and figure out what covers you want to do. We're going to try to to get everyone together in the next week or so to rehearse for the Wheeler Centennial in December.

I hadn't given that a thought either, how it was ten years since we got out of high school. At that point I didn't want to see any of my old classmates, and right then it included Artie. He always threw enough sweetness into his wild-ass schemes, which made them hard to refuse.

The bass is a beautiful thing, but this isn't a big enough bribe for me to play in front of people again.

SMUG began as part of the high school orchestra. Randy played the viola and Sparky played tympani or whatever percussion was needed at the time. That I played the stand-up bass was a joke, for a short, round kid to play a giant fiddle. Except I had a growth spurt so it worked out. Sparky just liked banging on things but Randy was a prodigy. He played completely by ear, pretending to read the music to fool old Mr. Proper.

The orchestra was better than expected, lacking the dissonance present in schools where kids only took orchestra to get out of gym. Proper, or "Mr. Propeller,' was a hard-ass. He chose pieces that weren't beyond our reach and practiced until it was pretty much perfect.

Randy was bored and wanted us to play something more modern, suggesting that the orchestra take a crack at the Moody Blues' "Nights in White Satin." The song is a sweet sample of symphonic rock that almost everyone likes. Propeller cut Randy off before he finished the question, saying if he were to play any popular music it would be from Frank Sinatra. But Nelson Riddle's arrangements were too complicated for our little group.

This took Randy from bored to pissed off, while he still pretended to be a good musical citizen. That was until the spring concert, when he began to add triplets and arpeggios to the once perfect arrangements. This threw everyone off, but Sparky and I were the worst offenders. We completely lost our place and began to improvise, sounding just like an orchestral Frank Zappa piece that we'd heard at Artie's house.

We all got kicked out that night. I was becoming competent at bass, but this was the first time that I had any fun in orchestra. It was natural, then, for us to meet up again a week later to play in the hotel ballroom.

It was then I learned that Randy and Sparky had been playing together for some time, making music that was somewhat less than orchestral. Sparky had a double-bass drum set bigger than anything I'd seen while Randy played a faded white triple pickup Gibson SG. He had a Marshall amp head and a homemade speaker cabinet. After a few minutes, it was clear that Randy could play everything pretty much like the record but chose to improvise. Hearing "Spirit in the Sky" at top volume and a raging solo gave the radio hit some balls.

Randy had a shit-ton of equipment. He had a reel-to-reel deck where he double tracked the bass and rhythm guitars. He also had a bass, a battered Gibson with a missing cutaway. For the sake of sound and appearance there was a Marshall bass amp and homemade stack.

"I don't know how to play bass guitar," I said. "Sure you do," Randy said. "You learn patterns and scales, throwing in whatever note fits. And you have to watch the drummer." He made it sound so simple. After a while, it was.

We took up residence in the ballroom every afternoon, drawing a bigger crowd each day. They opened up the bar, and we had a cool little happy hour club. The good news was that it was only a rehearsal, with stops and starts. The afternoon crowd likes to talk, and we didn't care if they were listening.

We played a mix of covers and Randy's originals, all instrumentals. We had no singer. We'd explain that to people and they'd always point out that Bob Dylan and Neil Young are great singers with different voices. No, we'd reply, we really can't sing.

Too bad, because Randy wrote some inspiring lyrics. Although I can't remember any of them right now.

So Lois was inevitable, if we were going to go any further. Randy spotted her at school playing somber versions of Joni Mitchell songs under a tree next to a parking lot. Randy asked her whether she wanted to sing something different.

She came to a few afternoon romps. One day she appeared carrying a yellow Hagstrom guitar. At that point we noticed a third Marshall mini-stack, a microphone, and a PA.

Her voice was odd, and unpredictable. It went from light and ethereal to a guttural snort in the same song. Many people heard two voices. Randy got compliments for his backup singing. He stayed silent, perpetuating the mystery.

We might play three in a row and then skip a week, but the crowd always showed up. We could have charged a cover, but we were selling a lot of soda pop. We didn't want to get greedy.

November 4

It's Sunday, with no chance of anyone calling for Cricket tech support. This might be the last quiet stretch before the product release date, scheduled for the middle of the month. I started writing stuff down as a way to learn the computer, so I know what I'm talking about. It was an exercise that meant nothing. I was sort of following Artie's plan. He said he learned how to use a database by entering information about every girl he met and how far she let him go.

And writing about SMUG helps clear the air about something that started badly and got so much worse.

Every week I asked Randy whether they couldn't find another bass player, since I wasn't anywhere close to the talent in the rest of the band. He would say no, there is no one in either Wheeler or the Notch who could play and who owned a bass guitar. I can't play, I would respond, and I don't own that damaged bass.

He would then change direction. No, you aren't that good at the bass but you know the songs and how we think. He said that groups succeeded because they communicated well with each other and worked as a team. Connection was more important than skill.

"Me and Sparky are pretty out there, playing ten notes or hitting ten beats when everyone else does four," he said. "When we played together as a duo it never got out of the house since we had no framework. You and Lois are the normal ones. You give us an anchor. Like a moon that revolves around the sun."

Moons don't revolve around suns but I didn't correct him. I knew what he meant.

"If you don't know what you're doing just take the root note of the chord we're on and play a pattern double time along with the beat," he said.

Artie wasn't exactly helpful. He couldn't play or sing but sure could talk. He started booking shows wherever he could, not always letting the club owners that we were all 16 years old. The state had just lowered the drinking age to 18 so it wasn't that far off, and we were all early bloomers when it came to outgoing teenage awkwardness.

Artie still looked like a little kid. He did most of his work on the phone so it didn't matter. Like booking us into bars. By the time people figured out how young we were it was too late to find anyone else.

Randy taped the rehearsals, times when no one was around and I could let go. He isolated the six best live takes, adding overdubs, and inserting sound effects. We had an audition tape that wasn't completely terrible. A few times I heard the bass line and wished I could play that well in front of people.

Our final performance was in Wheeler in September 1972. Artie had created the First Annual Wheeler Rock Festival, which was something of an overstatement. It was four bands on a single night, playing outside in crisp Autumn. The headliner was an up and coming performance artist who could sing and play. "You need to watch this guy," Artie said. "He will be the biggest rock star in the world within two years."

Maybe, maybe not. Artie described his music as dreamy and decadent, while the 'd' word that came into my mind was "derivative."

Artie insisted the Future Star was the real thing. He had read that his next album would catapult him into the front lines of the rock world. There was a theatrical tour to go along with the album the next year. Right now, the Future Star was playing practice gigs in small town America, fronting a crisp four piece band. It was the same configuration as SMUG: Drummer, bassist, lead guitarist and a lead singer who played rhythm guitar.

Artie had co-opted the Wheeler Amphitheater, which was generally used for summer pops concerts. It consisted of a wide red-brick stage at the bottom of the hill, surrounded by oak and maple trees. SMUG was the kickoff band. When we started The field was covered with mist, which lifted to reveal the fall colors. It was a short set, around 25 minutes, but we hit a peak on the last two songs. Maybe we really had something special here.

I grabbed a beer and cooled down, leaning on an equipment case backstage within view of the bass player. Maybe I could learn by watching. Randy was always pushing me toward a higher skill level, but this was the first time I ever wanted to improve my playing on my own.

"That was quite extraordinary." A voice on my left, out of nowhere. I turned to see a guy about my height with a narrow face painted white. He was wearing a kimono and a turban. The Future Star.

"Um, what?" I didn't acknowledge who he was. He already knew, presumably.

"You're quite young," he said. "But your little band sounds better than a lot of people I've played with."

"Thanks." I didn't know how to respond. I wished he would go away and talk to someone less nervous.

"Stretching out 'Spirit in the Sky,' was really inspired," he said about our final number. "The rest of the set was brilliant but this interpretation included something that has eluded me.

We had played the whole song and then kicked into a long instrumental section; Lois would play the chugging riff which I would amplify with a loud bass line. Not exactly musical rocket surgery. The Future Star heard a fifth sound that did not come from any of the instruments. It was a high pitched tone that followed the chord changes and made it sound as if everything were in a tunnel. He had a word for the new sound, "resonance."

How, he asked, did we do that?

Everything shifted, and I relaxed. He was no longer a creepy person that I wanted to go away so I'd be alone with my thoughts. He was an accomplished, intelligent being who was interested in my opinion. That felt good, since it didn't happen a lot.

"You're not the first one who's noticed," I said. "After our shows people always ask who is playing the organ. We always thought their hearing was shot. Or they were too high. Which made sense, because many these jams sound better when you're fucked up."

That was until someone mentioned the "Spirit in the Sky" in the same context of what the Future Star had just said. We talked about it, and Lois was the only one who remembered the performance.

Lois said the break went on for about eight minutes, double the usual. We three thought the jam was too short, worrying about giving the audience their money's worth. That lasted until we remembered that nobody paid to get in.

"The three of us basically lost consciousness," I said. "Randy always plays stoned but the other three are as sober as rocks. There are nights when we remember every excruciating minute of the closing jam."

"I thought the jam was superb," he said.

It was preparation time, and time for him to start his process. He told me that he had created a production company and had already recorded several albums with forgotten singers that were expected to boost them back into the limelight. All, I supposed, recorded through a filter of dreamy decadence.

He wanted to change direction, lending his name and skill to new bands.

"The first two albums were fun," he said of his recent production efforts. "But I got the feeling with all of them that I was in a dinosaur graveyard. The reanimation was bound to get me in trouble."

He gave me a card with no name, just ten digits. Call this number, he said. Did we have a demo tape? Yes, I said, but it didn't have any resonance. He told me to go fuck myself. I think he likes me. He told me the tape was a formality as he was already sure that he could make us a great record.

"Don't lose the card," he said. "If you call the label or my management you'll never get through."

Our performance that night was pretty great. We didn't want to practice or play anywhere else because it would dilute the experience. We only had to meet to consider next steps, and the four of us decided to meet at the café about a month after the show. Artie turned up like he was supposed to be there.

"We need to discuss next steps," Lois said. "That last show really worked but we need to take this seriously or give it up. You guys are great. I can't imagine having a better backup band. I want to see us in bigger places."

All of us bristled at "backup band" but kept it to ourselves.

"You guys are my best friends," I said. "But I don't want to do this. I like playing but the stress of getting there is too strong. If we had made a record or got famous or something I'd probably take an overdose and you'd have to replace me anyway. So let's get it over with."

The three of them jumped into motion. I was part of the band and part of the plan. I am essential to its foundation. There is a magic that occurs when we play together. We need to continue to find the resonance.

I switched to the backup plan.

"I talked to the Future Star after the last show," I said. "He wants to produce us. He said we could make a great record. He's a nice guy and really likes us. He heard the resonance. He gave me his secret number. But I don't want to do this anymore so I threw it away."

That did the trick. SMUG was shattered. Everyone left angry, and Artie didn't get to say a word. Which hadn't happened, ever.

What he would have said: He lifted two songs from the demo tape, "Cloud Pictures" and "Pretending." He remixed the recordings and released them on a single. Which was a surprise to all the former band members until they heard it on the radio.

November 6

I decided to take a day off from writing yesterday. I knew the phone wouldn't ring, and I am bored with my own story. I'm tempted to skip ahead to the interesting parts but that would be cheating.

Today some people came into the café asking about my father. I told them Walter was no longer with us. They expressed their sympathies, paid their check and left without saying much else.

I might have misrepresented the situation. Walter left town about four years ago, days after John Lennon was shot. Reagan was elected the month before. Combined, these two occurrences represented the end of the world as we know it. Or at least the end of the 1960s.

Walter went somewhere else. As far as we knew he is still there. One day he was ranting away against Reagan and guns, the next day he was gone. There was no warning, since he'd been threatening to leave the country in reaction to one political firestorm or another. His fury had subsided during the Carter years, either because he didn't hate the president so much or because he got a dog, a massively intelligent border collie mix named Ruby.

Ruby arrived as a puppy about two years before Walter left, a gift from an old girlfriend. Anyone else would have seen gifting an animal without the recipient's approval as an act of aggression, the gift that keeps on taking. Walter took to Ruby right away, spending the first year training her and the second teaching her to play chess. (Here, setting up the board and pointing to the piece that Ruby should knock over).

Walter had been threatening to leave for years. We knew he had followed through when we found that Ruby had disappeared as well.

I don't have a lot in common with Walter, aside from growing up in the same house. Which wasn't a house at all, just a maze of rooms and a changing cast of characters. Our first job was working on the hotel's cleaning team with the second working in the kitchen. Hazel, and then Walter always hired someone to run the .

Walter was drafted into the army and served in Korea. This deprived Hazel of her right hand so she decided to simplify. She turned the hotel into a resort operating from May to October. She wasn't giving anything up here as there weren't enough guests in the winter months to make the hotel worthwhile.

She established a one week minimum stay booked in advance. The guests were often old people, ranging from 40 to 70.

Walter changed in Korea. His attitude toward managing the property had evolved from petulant reluctance to speed and motivation. Hazel welcomed this, she was sick of being in charge.

After talking to Mrs. Babian I uncovered a family secret. Or at least a disturbing pattern. Arnold was the manager but Hazel—his romantic partner— did most of the work. Walter took that idea and added some variety. He would focus his attention on a hotel guest and after a few days would offer her a job as assistant manager and a new life as his one and only. There were three women who played that role from my first memories, around 1958, and when Walter walked out. The fourth one was Andy, who moved in six years ago. Walter wanted everyone to think he had "gone gay," never saying so directly but hinting that he was trying new experiences.

Walter and Andy would huddle in the café for hours sitting next to each other. They would often hug and kiss in public. But when they retired to the family wing they had separate apartments and never spent the night in each other's space. That I knew of.

It was a little strange, getting a new mom every few years. But I welcomed the variety and had no trouble letting go of one and welcoming the next. They all took an active interest in me, offering advice and answering my precocious questions. When I was 11 and full of biological wonderings it was Margaret who provided a reproductive roadmap.

People gossip, and I was always hearing how Walter abused and manipulated these poor women before leaving them high and dry. Most of this was behind his back, but if someone directly addressed it he said the women were here on their own free will. They could leave any time.

I knew why they stayed, because living in the Blue Notch Mountain House with Walter made them feel needed and special. There was plenty to do, but it all moved at 3/4 speed and was never too frantic. The customers accepted this, and did not eat at the if they had to be somewhere else in an hour.

People judged Walter for his visible fractured irrationality, but that is to dismiss his most compelling trait. He listened to people, actively. He looked them in the eye and responded with questions that moved the conversation along. He never looked over your shoulder to see who else was in the room. His responses were honest and probing, never obsequious. There was no false encouragement, If he didn't like it he would tell you why. You would walk away anxious to show him the next version.

So it made sense that women liked him and were attracted to the idea of moving in and helping out. His compliments were golden, as they felt like a blast of sunlight on your skin. They always came from your intellectual accomplishments. He offered no support to people who slid by on their beauty or heredity.

He was always there for my three moms. He might fly off the handle if they neglected an important chore or did it poorly, but they always knew that his affection was strong. Other women, tourists usually, observed these relationships and jumped to the conclusion that the couple wasn't solid because the woman was submissive and unhappy.

He didn't always turn his laser beam of love on me. If I was doing something nasty or wrong, like breaking into abandoned shacks, I could very easily tell him I was doing something else. He didn't seem to show that much interest as long as I was safe. When Mrs. Babian told me about Walter's real parentage and Hazel's dissembling about the topic I didn't let him know that I knew.

"I have grown very fond of you," Mrs. Babian told me the last time I talked to her. "But they have trouble with the truth. Hazel lied to her husband and her son about who fathered whom. Telling your father that his father died was especially cruel. Although by that point there was no chance that Jack was ever going to come back and prove her wrong."

She asked what I knew about my mother. I never knew her, I said. She died in childbirth. I came out healthy, but my stillborn twin was too much for her. She said I needed to look deeper and challenge Walter's version of events.

Mrs. Babian told me these stories as a serial. I may not visit for weeks, but we'd always pick up where we left off. She died before delivering the next chapter, upsetting me enough that I forgot to dig deeper into what she said. A year later, when I was in tenth grade, Walter took me aside for "something important." I assumed that I was getting a new mom.

"Your birth mother's not dead," he said. "She's running for congress."

Denise Collins was elected to a small rural district in upstate New York in the Bicentennial year that pulled a lot of Democrats into congress. The only national news she generated was in 1981 when Ronald Reagan was shot. Republicans had picked up many seats that year although the house was still controlled by the Democrats. She said that Reagan could not be killed by a bullet because he didn't have a heart. People on both sides pretended to be appalled by the statement. But it was all a sham. The Republicans were gleeful that a Democrat made such a stupid mistake and the Democrats privately agreed with what she said.

She didn't apologize. Four days after the shooting she was the lead story on national news.

"Yeah, I said it," she said. "But you're nuts if you think I really wished him physical harm. People say this kind of shit all the time about the other side. I just had the misfortune that someone overheard me.

"There is much frustration on Capitol Hill right now," she said. "We have a new administration that shows little respect for the environment and favors an increased defense budget over social programs. While our new president may not be a racist he has many racist friends, and these new Nazis are intent on riding his coattails into legitimate government positions. It's a frightening time for the country.

"Making malicious jokes about the opposition is part of the game. So I'm not going to apologize for this."

As a demonstration of this she told a joke, asking why cats walked around with their tails in the air.

"To show off their Reagan buttons."

As far as I know Denise Collins was the first politician to say "shit" on a national news program, followed by a discussion of cats' assholes. I wouldn't go as far to say that I was proud of my mom as those emotions were beyond me. But I then resolved to vote for her if I ever got the chance.

Walter didn't talk to be about Denise beyond disclosing that she was not dead. I didn't want to know the details, knowing that I'd never get the truth from him anyway. At the same time, I stopped feeling guilty about not telling him who his real father was.

One year ago Denise wrote me a letter, included here. Eight typed pages, single spaced. So I might rush ahead if it gets boring.

Dear Paul,

You might have heard of me. My name is Denise Collins. I am a native of New York State and serve as a representative of the 20th district in the United States Congress. I spent a year living in Blue Notch between high school and college staying with my mother, Madeline Babian. It was during that time I met your father. We had a relationship and I ended up giving birth to you before starting college and a career in law and politics.

I know that Walter told you I was dead and later changed his story to something closer to the truth. I am not writing to apologize for abandoning you, because that isn't what happened, and I can't say that I'm sorry for not being part of your life. Having a child when I was not yet 20 would have changed my life for the worse. I was born in when women were marginalized as housewives and were locked into that identity. My mother had escaped that, leaving my father when I was ten to move west and raise goats. She was there one day and gone the next, which wasn't easy for me. My father told me she died. When he died I learned the truth. My extended visit to my mother was an effort to get reacquainted, although it didn't work out the way either one of us would have liked.

I've made a decision that could involve you. After working in congress for seven years I've decided to take the next step and run for the senate. I'm not completely confident that I can beat the incumbent, but the people around me have convinced me to give it a shot. They know I'm restless in the House and believe I can go further. There is no downside, they tell me, if I run and lose I'll impress a lot of people and raise my visibility. Because I'm just that likable.

They call it a "win-win," which sounds like a stutter. I hope that stupid expression never catches on.

Here's where you could be involved: Politics has become personal, with each side throwing dirt at the other. It's like past times in our history, and it's just going to get worse. If I am successful at first my opponents—the Democrats before the primary and the Republicans after — will set their research bloodhounds free to sniff out any scandal. I'll be surprised if no one digs out your birth certificate, which has my name in white-on-black. They will then spin the story to make me look heartless and stupid. They will knock me first for having a baby out of wedlock, and second for selfishly abandoning him. They will point out that someone with low morals and disregard for family does not deserve to be in the Senate.

I made my choices that I don't regret. They felt right at the time. Had I acted differently I would be in a different space. I'm pretty sure that if I had spent my life in Blue Notch raising a child and running a hotel I'd be nuts by now. And you would not have escaped unscathed. Your life, I am certain, would not be as calm as it is today.

Other people in my position would try to manage the potential damage. Preemptively contact all the witness and providing a good cover story. That's against my nature. Beyond that, I would have no right to ask you to lie or tell a selective truth. If a reporter or political operative contacts you about this I hope, you are honest with your feelings. If your life was ruined by my abandonment say so. If you believe I owe you love, or money, share it with the world. By the same token, you should be free to say that you have forgiven me, or that you don't give a shit. What I did then doesn't say anything about who I am today. So if it goes public, bring it on and we'll deal with it.

With that in mind I want you to know my story, because I know whatever Walter has said has no relation to the truth. I don't know how much my mother told you, but I'm pretty sure she had her own biases.

I grew up in New York City. My father managed the tie department at the downtown Wheeler's store and my mother was an artist and a gardener. They couldn't reconcile their differences so mother left us one day. My father said she had sailed off to sea and her boat sank. The word "death" was never used but he didn't say anything to clarify things.

He jumped in front of a subway when I was 18, and I learned where mother had sailed off to. I finished high school and traveled west to see her. She had a lovely spot on the side of a hill and a dozen goats, all with names. At that point I couldn't tell one goat from another. After three weeks, I knew each one of them by smell.

I spent a lot of time in the Blue Notch because it was the only place to go. Maybe I was looking for a way to get into trouble and spread my young wings, as it were. I met Walter on that first day, and was immediately captivated. He had incredible charisma and warmth. And focus. He paid closer attention to me than my distant father, my abandoning mother, and everyone that I'd ever met in between.

Walter was just a year older than I was, so we connected as part of the same restless generation. I know this is a cliche, but it seemed that the 1950s were in black and white. Walter was the first full-color person I'd met. But while I was looking for an adventurous, enlightening fling before going out in the world Walter had different plans.

I would talk about college, and he would encourage me, but said nothing about where he would go to school. It took me a while to figure out that he had no plans to leave Blue Notch. Like his mother, his goal was to run the hotel as a way to provide a nice place to live and work. He didn't even like going down the hill to Wheeler for supplies and managed to delegate the trips whenever he could.

Two months after we started "keeping company" I found out I was pregnant. I wasn't happy about it, especially since I had made him wear condoms. I know that's a creepy detail to know about your parents, but it is an important part of the story.

The day I needed to tell him I was waiting in his apartment and decided to empty the trash. There were a few weeks worth of condoms in there. Each one had a little hole torn in the tip. So when I told him I was "with child", I was not as graceful as I could have been.

I felt betrayed, humiliated and lost. I retreated to my mother's house. She had some training as a midwife, enough to make sure the birth went smoothly. About three months later I was getting attached to you in a way that I wasn't going to able to pull away from. So one day I wrapped you up, dragged along a crib and a bag of diapers and took you to meet your papa.

His reaction was ecstatic, which was no surprise. Part of his plan was to anchor me down with a child, and to him. You were so damn cute, how could I resist? He knew I was trapped. He was wrong.

I tucked you away and brought out a bottle of wine. I loved Walter in my own way, so it wasn't that much of a masquerade. After he'd fallen asleep I got up and left. My mother was outside, and she drove me to the airport.

I've not looked back with regret for many reasons. If I had gotten pregnant because of my own carelessness, I would have taken some of the responsibility. But I was lied to and used as a breed mare. If this story gets out those who would hurt me will wail about how I don't have the motherly instinct, which is necessary for any woman to feel compassion.

The truth is; I'm missing the parenting gene. I'm in spitting distance of 50 years old and have never felt the biological clock tick away. I've also never been married or seen in public with a man, at least since I've been elected. So they'll certainly try to cast me as gay, or worse.

I know this going on forever. If you are like Walter, you stopped reading about 30 lines in. If you've read this far I want you to know that I think of you often and wish you well. Don't worry though, it's not to the point where I want to meet you and have a "relationship." I remember how disturbing it was meeting my dead mother when I was 18, and don't think it would be any easier for you when you are 28. We've learned how to live with each other, and I don't see the need to change that.

It's late, I've been doing this for hours. But I don't feel like stopping for some reason. The wine is part of it, I finished one bottle and started another. I'm starting to mix up my words and will stop here in case I get too sentimental and decide I want to come out and see you before the campaign announcement. After that I will have no time to myself at all. Probably for the rest of my life.

Wherever this goes is OK with me. If you need to see me, I won't run away. If I get elected president and you want to start a beer company and cash in on my name I'll help where I can. Just keep in mind that I know we are connected. Whether we talk or not won't change that.

I also want you to know that I saw you at my mother's funeral. You were a junior in high school, I think. I was going to talk to you but was distracted by an eagle carrying a squirrel. By the time it flew away you were gone.

Best wishes,

Denise

My response was less epic.

Dear Denise;
Thanks for writing. It was cool how you could just open up to the page and write honestly and from your heart. I'm sure I'll never be able to pull that off.

Walter told me you were dead when I was small but slipped out the truth when you ran for congress the first time. I saw you on TV and decided that I would vote for you some day. Since I'm not moving to New York, or anywhere else in the foreseeable future, you're going to have to run for president for that to happen.

Since you are being honest—when I see you on TV or read about you in the papers I get a warm feeling. Pride? Not really, I don't think. I like the way you talk and act, and feel good those attitudes are in me, somewhere.

But I agree there is no reason for us to meet. It would be different if I thought of you as the abandoning mother, or you eternally regretted giving me up. So it's better for us to stay where we are and maintain these warm feelings than to meet and be annoyed by each other's quirks and flaws.

So everything's fine. I hope that you will let me know who you are if you ever come out here again. In the same way, if I'm ever on the east coast or in New York I'll make it a point to call. But as you may have heard, I've only left the area once.

Take care,

Paul

Reagan won by a landslide, Denise lost by a whisker. That night the election reporters said that Denise Collins was the type of person Reagan needed to recruit for his second term. She was attractive, articulate, and a Democrat, so she'd certainly help to widen his base.

November 7

Lois blew town right after SMUG folded, enrolling at Goddard College in Vermont, a modern education paradise. After two years, she transferred to the Berklee College of Music for voice and guitar. She moved to New York City and hooked up with a modern dance group. After a few years, she formed a band, a five piece like SMUG with a keyboard. She called the band "Anita," after a cheerleader from high school and for the word play possibilities.

Her stage presence was electrifying, with classical patterns and dance incorporated into the performance. Her voice moved from light to dark and back again. The songs were twisty but were anchored by a rock beat. Whether she meant it or not Lois had not ditched her SMUG roots.

I'd seen her on TV, "Saturday Night Live" and bought her first album called *Anita: Name.* She had renamed herself after the band, which was all female while the others were credited with their first names. Or maybe their made up names.

The record was sold in the Wheeler department stores and the Notch's small shop, but the local connection was unexploited. It hadn't been that long, but no one seemed to recognize our Lois.

I hadn't talked to her since she stormed out of rehearsal nearly ten years ago. When the phone rang this morning I knew her voice right away and didn't make her identify herself.

The conversation went something like this:

"Hi."

"Hey. It's nice to hear from you. I have your album."

"Thanks. I should have sent you a copy. If you weren't the best bass player you helped me to jump start my songwriting, and my new band still aspires to some of that SMUG resonance."

I didn't mind being characterized as "not the best" bass player, since I never thought I was any good at all.

There was no small talk or get acquainted chatter. I remembered her habit of getting right to the point.

"Yeah, something really strange happened this morning. I went out to move the band's van from one side of the street to the other when I found a piece of construction paper with 'SMUG must stay dead" painted on. It was face down on the windshield and left a mark. I've spent all morning scraping it off. I didn't quite get it all."

"I got one too, earlier this week," I said. I didn't think much of it. It doesn't mean much to me, as there is no way SMUG will ever get back together, considering how famous you're getting. This is a dumb-ass idea, on Artie's part."

"I was actually considering it," she said. "The band is touring next year, and I thought it would be cool if SMUG opened a few dates. Artie says he has nearly enough tracks for an album. We could record a few more. It would be a lot of fun, I thought, until I got this."

I told her that this little threat didn't change my mind about playing together again. I was against it before and was more against it now. I didn't know what "SMUG must die" or "stay dead" meant, but I was sure it wasn't a good thing.

"Come on, it would be fun," she said. "It would get you out of that hotel and into the sunlight. And don't tell me that you are working. You must know that your so-called boss, Artie, is behind this whole reunion idea."

"So you're not scared off?"

"A little. But I feel that SMUG didn't end well, or naturally. We had a little bit of magic. Imagine if "Cloud Pictures " came out when we were still together and we promoted it. It would have been a bigger hit, and at this point in your life you could tell people that you made one great single that everybody heard."

We had yet to address why SMUG split. We didn't so much break up as I blew the whole thing apart.

"Let me ask you a question," she said. "If we had allowed you to leave the band would you have given us the Future Star's number?"

"I'm not so sure I would use the word 'allow,'" I said. "I told you what I wanted to do, which was to quit the band. I was going to do it anyway. If I had given you the number, you or Artie or the other two would have bullied me into staying. I would say that I wanted out and would be asked to do just one more thing. Play on this song. Go to that recording session. Play this one show.

"When I say no to something people don't hear or believe it. I felt strongly about this and gave you the opportunity to let me go and find another bass player.

Your reaction convinced me that wouldn't happen gracefully. So no, I probably wouldn't have passed it on."

"You probably did us a favor," she said. "We might have made a record and gone on tour with the Future Star, but probably would run out of ideas after an album or three. Or we would have been dragged down when Future Star flamed out to became Burnout Star. I don't know where you guys would have ended up, but I would never have made it to college. I wouldn't have worked on my craft for years, and Anita would have a lot less depth and range."

She asked me whether I had heard from Sparky or Randy. Both of them lived in Wheeler, and both had received the "threat." Artie got one as well, and the three of them met the other day to discuss any next steps. But they got drunk and abandoned the agenda.

"Those two play in a cover band in the mainland," I said, using our nickname for Wheeler. "I don't think it's very successful because they still have day jobs. I do know that Randy's gotten better, which is hard to believe considering what he whipped up while he was playing in SMUG."

"He was really something," she said. "I was thinking of asking him to tour with me, but we want to keep it all female for now."

We had run out of things to say, and I needed to get to work.

"Um, there's one more thing," she said. "Did you get what I sent?"

"No, I haven't checked the mail in a week or two."

"It's an article about me—the band— from the Village Voice. I thought they were doing a complimentary profile of the new album, but it turned out to be an ambush. They outed me, found out about 'Lois Hannah' and asked all these snarky questions about SMUG. I lost control, and would have walked out of the interview if it wasn't at my own house."

The main point, she said, is that she had some harsh words for me specifically for losing the telephone number. The context statement, that the loss of that opportunity led to more fulfilling ones, was omitted from the article. She didn't want me to be mad or hurt. I didn't respond, but wondered why she didn't just let it go. There was no way I was going to see anything from the *Village Voice* out here.

"I want you to know that I forgive you for this and I want to be friends again," she said. "I think that it was a good thing you lost the number."

I told her that I hadn't really lost it and could mail it to her if she were interested. She stayed quiet for a second and then hung up. So much for "friends again."

November 8

The *Voice* was in my mail slot, in a huge wrinkled sloppily addressed envelope. I read about four paragraphs in, confirming that the old "any press is good press" notion is bullshit.

'Anita' Identity Change is More Than Skin Deep

By Ianthe Goldschweig

The singer known as Anita is waiting at the elevator when I arrive at her loft, offering a cup of fresh espresso brewed from the large red machine in her kitchen.

"We painted it red and decorated it with Christmas lights," she said. "That way if one of us gets up at night and needs to pee we don't trip over anything."

Anita lives in the wide open space with four other women, known only as Alice, Adrian, Allison, and Andrea. Each roommate has her own living space adjoining a common rehearsal area. The roommates aren't here, and a follow up call fails to learn their last names, or if these are their real names at all.

The four, along with Anita-the-woman, comprise "Anita," the band. After an exciting but unpolished debut, last year's Anita: Name they will soon release the more assured Anita: Hand The straightforward music belies an infatuation with cheap puns, but the possibilities are endless. Anita: Love. Anita: Fix. Anita: Break. And so on.

"Someday I'd like to put out a record called Anita: Fuck," Anita-the-woman said. "It should probably be a live album."

Both of the band's records are compelling, yet don't come anywhere near their live sound. On the album covers, Anita-the-woman draws the visual focus as her compatriots orbit around her image. The onstage dynamic changes the equation. Rhythm guitarist Anita, playing a bright yellow Hagstrom (a brand known only to guitar cognoscenti) bonds with Allison, the bass player, to supply the chugging instrumental foundation for each song. Drums, guitar and keyboards then swirl around them, alternating between sounds that play with and against the bass/guitar foundation.

Anita's voice (she is the band's only singer) is also a volatile element. Her higher range sounds like she's inhaled helium while the lower end borders on the masculine.

The highlight of their live show, and perhaps the most compelling reason for "Anita: Fuck," is an endless rendition of Norman Greenbaum's 1969 Jesus-Freak hit "Spirit in the Sky." The extended instrumental midsection becomes a battle between Andrea's keyboards, sounding like a church's pipe organ, and Adrian's demonic, dissonant lead guitar. A duel between good and evil that is won or lost, depending on the night.

Anita is dismissive when asked about these musical/ philosophical battles.

"We're just jamming," she said.

Anita-the-woman is not a very good interview. She speaks in short, precise sentences that answer the question and little more. She is an obstructionist, not wanting to divulge the personal details that the general public by nature craves about any new artist. If I were to bring this up she would no doubt let fly a cliche, like "I'm nervous around the press" or "I speak through my music."

So I try a different tack.

"Who is Lois Hannah?" I ask.

The cigarette that is destined for her mouth stops in mid air.

"You already know the answer to that question," she said, after a short pause. "I don't see why you had to be so sneaky about this."

I have done my homework. Lois Hannah is Anita-the-woman's given name. Both are 28 years old. They were born and raised in a western town called Wheeler, leaving just after high school graduation in search of life's great intangibles. They studied dance, music, and art, not earning any degrees but gaining mastery of each one in a short time.

"Lois's pool of knowledge was more like a reservoir," a college friend who now writes advertising copy told me. "It was very wide, and extremely deep. Everyone else had intelligence puddles."

She moved to New York in the late 1970s, Most starving artists work as waitresses or dishwashers while awaiting their big break but she broke the mold. She began working at the perfume counter in Wheeler's downtown store, a job she secured through her home town connections. She kept working until the release of Anita's first album.

While she had changed her public persona to "Anita" some time before she was always "Lois" to the shoppers. She didn't tell anyone about her other identity and no customer has remarked about this intersection, according to her former boss on the perfume counter.

"Lois was one of our best salespeople," her manager said. "She's bright, pretty, and smells great naturally. She never told customers what she did—or didn't wear when it comes to perfume."

In high school, Lois sang in a band called SMUG, all caps. They were headed for the big time according to Artie Connors, a fellow student who managed the band, but broke up after a fierce internal argument. "I don't remember what it was about," he said. "But Lois hasn't talked to any of the other three since she walked out of the room that night."

People still remember SMUG fondly, but a band end can change perceptions, like a local team who failed to win the state championship, Connors said. They did release one posthumous single, "Cloud Pictures" backed by "Pretending," that was a regional hit that stalled because there was no band to promote it.

"Cloud Pictures" is one of those irresistible songs that would have knocked then popular songs like "Billy Don't Be A Hero" and "You're Having My Baby" out of the box. It is full of 1960s cliches, a driving bass and jangly rhythm, blended with shimmering guitar, and 12-beat-to-the-measure drums. For a comparison you might visualize Jimi Hendrix and Keith Moon. All the cliches add up to its own entity, a song that you swear you've heard before but can't remember where.

The flip side is a little less exciting, starting softly with Lois/Anita singing "Pretending I like you so I don't have to strike you." Similar lines are repeated, each adding an instrument or a new sound. After one minute it's chaos, with her howling "Pretending to need you, not wanting to feed you" and other nonsensical phrases that follow the pattern. This results in a hypnotic sound although it obviously was made up on the spot.

Connors said that he wants to release the single along with a handful of other album tracks as an EP, but everyone has to agree first. Lois/Anita is a long shot since she is on a roll and probably doesn't want to interfere with her active career trajectory.

"I think people will want to hear this," Connors said of the proposed EP. "Although they'll certainly be more excited if some unreleased Beatles stuff ever surfaces."

"You already know the answer to that question," Lois/ Anita said. "It's not unusual for artists to create a new persona as they grow. I did leave that life, that world, as soon as I could. I created this art, and this image. 'Lois' isn't who I am right now, inside or out."

She talks about SMUG, making it clear that she'd rather not. The band was first formed with a drummer and guitarist, respectively Sparky Kendrick and Randy Powell. A third friend, known only as Paul the Hamster, was on bass although he was new to the instrument. He was recruited, she said, mostly because he lived in an old hotel that included cavernous practice spaces.

The three bonded when they were kicked out of the school orchestra, where Lois played triangle. She would have rather joined the chorus, but "my voice was too weird; they didn't know to make me a soprano or an alto."

She was a bit of a showoff in school as she knew more than anyone else there. She read voraciously, gaining enough knowledge to stay at least three grades ahead of her classmates.

She had the same turned up nose and know-it-all expression, causing a school bully to tag her as "A smug little bitch." It was the same bully who had slapped the bassist with the "hamster" moniker. For a time they considered calling themselves "Smug Hamster" but gave up because no one would get the joke (the bully had disappeared from school shortly after naming his victims). So they became SMUG, all caps.

SMUG built a local rabid fan base, like every other marginally original small town rock combo. She said the fans never got to hear the good stuff, as about 65 percent of their performances were in front of small or nonexistent groups.

"Paul was an inspired bass player, after all," she recalls. "He was never confident in his abilities, and always wanted to quit. He played patterns instead of improvising, which worked perfectly because Randy and Sparky were so wild."

She admits borrowing this formula for her next band. But while the SMUG configuration was an accident, she deliberately recruited a solid bass player and a trio of wild musical horses.

Hamster had a tragic flaw. He was spot-on in rehearsal, but had to be pushed onstage for any performance outside of the hotel. Once persuaded his patterns and fills were stiff and uncomfortable. She said the audience didn't care because "no one notices the bass player unless he really sucks or is too loud."

Hamster's stage fright flaw was understandable, but the sabotage was a capital offense. SMUG last and largest show was its best, she said, the band managed to click despite the presence of a large audience. The solution was for Hamster to just turn his back. After the show, the band had the opportunity of a lifetime when the headliner paid them a grand compliment and offered to produce their album. Except he approached Hamster, who deliberately lost the number.

"I was very bitter for a long time," she said. "I haven't been home since. Now that I put it in perspective I think Hamster did me a favor. He made me start at the bottom and create out of nothingness. He made me face the competition and prevail. I'm not going to thank him for this, since his actions came from pure selfishness."

We tracked down Hamster at his home in Wheeler's Notch and asked him about SMUG. His response was cryptic, saying he had never heard of Denise Collins and his mother was dead. It must be sad to have been left behind, and to be out of sync with the world.

She acknowledges that she is better off in the long run, but feels for her former bandmates.

"If we had put out an album then we would be a musical footnote today," she said. "We were too young. But it was probably the only chance Randy and Sparky had to do something with their lives."

How does she feel about the possibility of the SMUG tapes release, as proposed by Artie Connors?

"I've never heard them aside from the single and can't imagine them being any good," she said. "If someone likes my current work, they most likely will find SMUG primitive and derivative. But if Randy and Sparky, along with Hamster and Artie want to put it out, that's fine with me."

She relights her cigarette.

"Can I be Anita now?"

She didn't seem any happier about my next topic, whether women are finally achieving rock and roll parity. My asking the question makes it worse, or ensures that it won't get any better soon.

"You ask me how I compare with Madonna, Cyndi Lauper, or the Go-Go's," she said. "I swear I will give up what's left of my virtue to the first journalist who asks how I compare to Tom Petty or Michael Jackson."

The answer, she said, is that comparisons are unfair. The only things that matter are if the music is any good and it moves the listener. Another cliche.

"The Beatles were great because they never repeated themselves," she said. "I heard they would throw stuff away if it was too close to what they did before. That doesn't happen anymore, because a lot of the songs have

*been written and one song can very easily sound like
another. They are embedded in our subconscious.
Conceivably I could start playing an obvious song like "I
Can See for Miles" and think that I'd written it."*

*Anita: Hand is currently ready to go and will be
released in time for the Christmas season. Rehearsals for
a spring tour opening for Dire Straits will begin at that
time. Up until now the band has rehearsed in the loft,
which has drawn a mixed reaction from the neighbors. As
did a complete run-through of Anita: Hand on the
building's roof on a sunny October day.*

*"We were hoping that we'd get arrested or shut down,
like the Beatles' 'Let it Be' rooftop concert," she said.
"But everyone in the neighborhood thought it was a
regular rehearsal. The complainers didn't bother because
it never made any difference before."*

*The whole concert was filmed, anticipating police
conflict but that never happened. They are now "stuck"
with a pretty decent performance film that could be
shown in theaters or marketed to the burgeoning home
video market.*

*"I think we have something here," she said. "We draw
from the past in an original way. People don't ever take to
something completely new, but we have found a balance.
You think that you've heard our music before, but it is out
of sync enough to create new sensations."*

November 10

Yesterday I was sitting in the café contemplating
recent eventfulness when a beat up blue school bus pulled
up in front to the lodge. Two people emerged, one tall and
lanky along with a redheaded human spark plug. They
loaded large black boxes onto a wheeler and came into
the hotel lobby's front door. They headed to the rear
ballroom where SMUG last performed and opened the
boxes.

They assembled a full-size drum kit and a Marshall stack, right next to where my bass rig had somehow materialized. There was also a PA system, out of place because none of us sang. Randy was fondling his white triple-pickup Gibson SG, the same guitar he played during SMUG's first life.

I gave them a few minutes. I wasn't anxious to get this started.

I hadn't seen Randy or Sparky since the night SMUG broke up. We used to pass each other on the street all the time but that suddenly stopped happening. I can't speak for them, but every time I noticed them get out of a car or turn down a supermarket aisle I'd scatter.

Randy and Sparky worked in Wheeler. I haven't left the Notch in three years now, managing to get everything I want right here. So the chances of our meeting slimmed even further.

I skipped my morning routine. I'd "log on" through a "modem" to something called the Source, which connected to the AP wire. I liked to bounce around the various categories, reading news from another place. Sometimes the news from a state or a small town had detail that the networks skipped. This was the coolest thing about the computer, that you don't have to leave the house to get the news.

I don't worry about how long I'm searching, as Artie is footing the $5 hourly tab. After this little Cricket project fails I'll keep the machine around for the connection, although I'll probably have to pay my own way.

When Randy and Sparky heard me walk in they stopped setting up and practically ran over to me, shaking my hand and giving tentative hugs. It made me cringe, but I couldn't find a polite way to push them away.

"I am so glad we are all doing this," Randy said. "I'm pumped that Lois is participating, but I'm more pumped that you are on board so we can start again where it all left off."

Sparky playfully smacked my arm and laughed but didn't say anything. I remembered how Randy always spoke for Sparky who was either painfully shy or not very bright.

"Sure, man," I said. "This will be great just like before." I didn't point out how "before" ended, or recollect our last meeting when I blew up the band so it wouldn't continue. Because I didn't want to do this. I still don't want to do this.

Randy pulled two pieces of yellow construction paper. I recognized the virulent anti-SMUG messages.

"We both got these," Randy said. "It was kind of scary, since it turned up on the windshield of my car, which was locked in the garage. Sparky found his inside a drum case that hasn't been opened for years."

He slapped me on the back and gave me another hug.

"But it hasn't scared us away. Artie had already told us about the idea to get back together for Notch Days. We hadn't decided, but this convinced us.

"SMUG will not die. It will live on."

I told him that Artie had brought over the bass less than two weeks ago, and I hadn't taken it out of the case. He told me that didn't matter, that I would be great. I was always great.

It starts again. I express reluctance, or disinterest, or revulsion, and he just tells me I'm wrong. I end up going along, and being dragged away. I expect it will be a similar situation if an avalanche ever wipes out the Notch.

"We'll be ready in about fifteen minutes," he said. "You can go what you need to do and come back whenever. We'll just be tuning up and jamming. Take your time."

I tried to remember if I had heard about this somewhere, if there were messages I missed, or I wasn't listening in the first place. Somewhere along the line someone had said "yes" to setting up the ballroom as SMUG reunion central, presumably until next month's performance.

"Artie," I said aloud. "What the fuck?"

I didn't hear any loud noises after a while so I headed back about an hour later. Randy was smoking while Sparky was wearing headphones and assaulting a semicircle of rubber drum pads.

"I figured that would bring you back." he said.

"What would?"

"Silence. If we started playing, you'd stay away for sure. If there was no sound you'd be in to investigate."

Busted.

"I know you don't really want to do this," he said. "And I also get what you did the first time. We weren't listening to you. And we were selfish. We knew we wanted to take this as far as we could and figured once we had any kind of success you'd start digging it."

Randy was always flip and dismissive. This was the first time I'd ever had a serious conversation with him, about anything.

"If you really want to bail I understand," he said. "We can figure out some way that this won't work out. There's not a lot to do around here in the winter. But we need you for this to work. You won't have to leave home, and you can control how often we practice. Just get through the performance. If you really want out then that's fine. I'm sure Lois can convince the bass player from Anita to fill in."

He took the point home.

"Seriously. One show and you're out. No expectations. I promise you that, and Sparky is my witness."

Sparky threw his sticks up, caught them and winked at me, without skipping a beat.

"Sure, I'll give it a shot," I said. "But not today, OK?"
I invited them into a rear table in the café for a beer, even
though it was only 11:30.

Sparky still hadn't said a word.

Randy was always tall, so he didn't have to worry
about David Steel and his constituents. This proved the
stupidity of the average bully, because he was always
wispy and waif-thin. Any of those bruisers could knock
him over, but it was as if he were so far up in the
atmosphere that he was invisible to them.

In high school, we had our own little misfits table,
The four SMUG members were joined by a revolving
cast of losers and loners. None of them would stay very
long, although we tried to be friendly. Most of the other
kids avoided us and made it a point to give us some room.

"Hey, did any of you guys fart?" Lois asked one day.
"Everybody's keeping their distance, more than usual."

We told ourselves we didn't care and welcomed
ostracization from these jerks. In private, we would have
all admitted that it wouldn't suck if things were a little
warmer.

A few years ago one of the snotty cheerleader chicks
came into the with her parents. I watched from a back
table, figuring she wouldn't pay more attention to me than
she did in school. But she came over to my table with a
nervous hello. My invitation to sit down was
unacknowledged.

"You guys, in high school," she stammered. "You
were so cool and smart. We all wanted to talk to you and
be part of your fun. We loved hearing you play, and a lot
of us girls wished that you guys would ask us out. Some
of us, I mean them, wished Lois would ask us out."

In case I misunderstood she told me that she was in
college and engaged to a quarterback or somebody. In
case I tried to make up for lost time.

"Yeah, everyone liked Randy," I said. "It was nice
seeing you."

Randy wasn't more interesting than any of us, except maybe Sparky. Everyone liked him because he was a wizard on guitar. He could sound like anyone, but loved to play like Jimi Hendrix. He'd never do an actual Hendrix song, but blast out a wall of incomprehensible noise that somehow made sense. Like Hendrix (I'm told, because I never actually saw him play) Randy's hands would glide over the strings in gymnastic formations that would be impossible to imitate. You only knew he was playing because his hand motions corresponded to the wall of sound.

He could play slide like Duane Allman and solos like Eric Clapton. The sound was authentic but a little out of sync, enough so you knew that it wasn't Hendrix or Allman or anyone else.

Randy never went to college, although he could probably have earned a music degree with not that much effort. He worked as a library page in high school, shelving books, and moved up to a clerk's position right after high school. He'd worked there ever since high school and played the guitar on weekends. This was enough for a while, but he was getting a little restless.

Sparky had a job in the basement of a tire center. A pneumatic tube would shoot down an order. He'd fetch the correct tires and set them on a lift that led to the garage. He learned the inventory, knowing exactly where each tire was located. This allowed him to create a recess in a stack of tires, large enough for a bed and a TV. While this was once a dream job, he was also ready to move on.

"This was fun," Randy said, getting up from the table. "We're all set up here and can come back whenever you're ready. Just give me a call and we'll take the first cable car."

The cable car hadn't worked since the 1930s, or ever, but I got his point.

November 12

All these years I was sure Randy hated me. I was a little flipped out by his warm response, like the argument never happened. Randy couldn't subsume his nature, and was always going to push his vision on other people. He knew best, at least musically. That he was usually right made the arguments futile.

He was cordial and considerate. I spoke, and he listened. He didn't have Walter's laser-esque conversational focus, but it was way better than before. Proving that the ten years after high school should hold more than a weight gain and improved grooming habits.

His visit was a blur, so there were two things I didn't notice until he left. His hair was a bright blonde, and there was a "National Brotherhood Week" button on his guitar strap.

Everyone perceives their eighth grade year as pure hell. Mine really was. I was in my second year at Wheeler High School, a specially configured torture cauldron that included seven grades under one roof. We were all so excited to enter seventh grade the year before, but the bliss evaporated before lunchtime. There was a steady stream of older boys who took verbal and physical potshots at us, and pretty girls wouldn't look us in the eye.

"This is part of tradition," Randy said. "You get here, and the older kids kick the shit out of you until about ninth grade when they start picking on the new seventh graders. At that point it's our job to join in and torture the little shits."

Not me, I said. You will, he answered.

As part of our orientation we all got a Wheeler High baseball hat and bright yellow buttons emblazoned with "Class of 1975." I wore mine, which prompted derision from my peers. One day I was watching the cheerleaders practice, especially drawn to a girl with short red hair named Anita. She smiled throughout the routine, directly at me.

After practice, she stumbled toward the coach who handed her a pair of glasses. The smile wasn't for me. More to the point, she couldn't even see me. I still thought she was kind, and very pretty. One day I saw her teaching cheering routines to a group of seventh grade girls who were all at rapt attention. It was the first time I saw Lois, who was front and center with an open mouth and glazed eyes.

I had a different lunch period than Artie, Randy and Sparky, somehow ending up with all the older kids. After I didn't respond to the taunting they pretty much left me alone, although my knees would quake when I took my tray to the dishwashing station.

One day I was reading "Animal Farm" when Anita sat at my table.

"So how did you end up with all these assholes?" she asked.

"I don't know."

"I grew up with those guys," she said. "They're all harmless and not especially smart. If they ever start railing on you just wait and don't respond. They'll lose interest soon enough. What's your name?"

"Paul."

"That's a nice button, Paul. Can I try it on?"

"Sure."

I was struck dumb by her beauty, poise and confidence. I was pondering what to say when she got up and straightened her pleated plaid skirt.

"We're going steady, but don't tell anybody," she said, walking away.

Randy and Sparky didn't believe me. Randy's logic was flawless: "If you are going steady how come she doesn't eat lunch with you every day? And why doesn't she wear your pin?"

I resisted the impulse to respond to the jerks who yelled "Hey, Hamster, where's your fairy pin" but they lost interest in that line of questioning after a day or two.

Years later, after Anita had graduated, I wondered if her "commitment" to me was only a way to make me look slightly less ridiculous.

We arrived on a cold February Friday of my eighth grade year greeted by a giant "National Brotherhood Week" banner across the school. We didn't have to wonder about it very long, as we were immediately hustled into the gym for a full-school assembly. Dr. Warren, in his first year as principal, was standing in the middle of the gym floor with a microphone, next to Mrs. Britting, the head guidance counselor.

Having to deal with seven grades worth of students was difficult on a regular day, made worse by them suddenly landing all in the same room.

Everyone jumped when Dr. Warren said "attention please" as the microphone was turned way up.

"This is National Brotherhood Week, where we all learn to coexist with and understand each other," he began, as the volume decreased. "Here in Wheeler we do not see firsthand the institutionalized racism that is all too common in the rest of the country, but that doesn't mean we can't learn what it's like.

"Next week we are creating an environment similar to the segregated south of our too-recent history. You may notice that we have only a few black students here, and we didn't want to make things too close to current events." He said that blonde students would be forced to use the cafeteria entrance closest to the outside doors. They will be required to ride in the back five rows of every school bus. If there are not enough seats, they will have to stand.

"You will adhere to your regular class schedule, although blonde students must sit in the back of the classroom. Class curriculum will be unchanged, although Mrs. Britting and the rest of the counseling staff will visit each social studies class to hear what you are thinking and feeling.

"One week from today at 2 p.m. we will all meet here again, when select students and instructors will discuss what they have learned and how their lives will or will not change because of this experiment.

"I believe this will teach you some valuable lessons and be an example to other schools as to how learning doesn't always occur in a classroom."

My hair is dark brown so I wasn't part of this particular minority. I didn't think this was going to be a big deal. I wasn't going to treat my blonde friends any differently. Or I wouldn't, if I had friends who were blondes. Artie and I had the same dark hair, while Sparky and Randy were dusty brown.

"This might not completely suck," Artie said. "Maybe the greaseballs will pick on someone else for a change and we'll have a few days off."

Of the 800-or-so kids in the school about 25 percent had some shade of blonde hair. On Monday that ratio changed. About sixty usually blonde kids arrived with dark tresses. Some looked like professional dye jobs while others were just streaks of black or brown shoe polish that unconvincingly darkened their appearance.

"Cowards," I thought, knowing that any black person facing discrimination can't join the privileged class with hair dye or shoe polish.

Randy and Sparky, however, had dyed their hair bright blonde.

The blonde "greaseballs," as Artie called them, were part of the shoe polish crowd, while a few of them had taken the step of shaving their head. This was a yearly ritual for them, signaling that trouble was around the corner and hippies beware.

Instead of picking on the small, the weak, or someone who was just in their way they focused on blondes, with a new ferocity. Their usual viciousness ran up another notch. Their interpretation was that bullying was not only sanctioned by the school but encouraged.

At Monday lunch, a small blonde kid named Pat Reilly was beaten severely and taken to the hospital. On Tuesday morning, there was an all out rumble between the bullies and members of the football team. Only four of them were blonde, but they decided to stick together and protect their teammates. This time the faculty attempted to get involved, but none of the participants would rat out the others, no matter what side they were on.

Tuesday afternoon a reporter and a photographer from the local paper visited English class, interviewing three kids: Mary and Peter who had dyed their blonde hair brown to avoid conflict, and myself talking about the lack of resistance and protest against the new rules. "They are all acting like a bunch of Uncle Toms," I opined.

My classmate Peter Meller, who had died his dark blonde hair a darker brown, justified his lily-livered action.

"I had never seen real discrimination before and wanted to observe rather that to be directly involved," he spouted. "I think that we learned what prejudice was and how to avoid it."

On Wednesday, we were all on the front page of the paper. The fence in front of the school was decorated with "Kill the Blundes" in red spray paint. In fifth period classes, just after lunch, our teachers all read a statement from Dr. Warren:

"The National Brotherhood Week experiment is cancelled, effective immediately. All the signs will be removed by the end of the day, but students are now free to travel through all areas of the school unrestricted. We are taking this action because we feel the lessons have already been taught. I am proud of the students, because they have already found out what it was to be discriminated against. There will, however, be no assembly on Friday. Thank you."

"And me, with all this hideous blonde hair," Randy moaned. "Maybe we could start a petition to get them to reconsider."

"Sure," I said. "Maybe the blonde kids will sign up for another two days of getting the shit kicked out of them."

An article in the Friday paper about the cancellation of the project, relating to upperclassmen Dan and Jack Kirkman. The (dark haired) brothers lived with their mother in a mansion styled house just south of Wheeler while their father, Dan Kirkman Sr., represented us in the U.S. Congress. Dan Sr., was well liked by his family and friends, since he represented the citizens of Wheeler as staunch supporters of President Richard Nixon. It turned out that Dan Sr. had pulled his nose far enough out of Nixon's butt to send Dr. Warren a telegram, calling for an immediate cessation of this "dangerous" experiment.

"I resent the fact that they are planting the idea of prejudice in our children," he wrote. "I have struggled to keep my children from learning prejudice, which is too serious to play games with.

Kirkman also wrote "there is a Negro woman who lives in my home, eats at my table and is accepted as a member of my family."

It only took a few hours before the bullies shifted their attention from the blondes and back to where it belonged, to the people they pushed around before. They added Pete Meller and the other cowards who went dark for the week found it wasn't easy to return to their natural shade.

"I don't care what color your hair is," I overheard alpha bully Eddie Kerrigan say as he tripped Meller. "You'll always be a pussy."

I called Randy on Saturday morning and told him to come on up anytime. He was there at noon and began tuning up; the bass, drums and his three guitars. He called for us a half hour later, and we spontaneously began playing a slow version of the three-chord masterpiece "Gloria."

"Alright, let's start with the obvious." Randy said, chugging on a crisp A chord that morphed into a C-D progression on the third and fourth beats of the second measure.

It was "Spirit in the Sky," the SMUG showpiece appropriated by Anita-the-band and the song that had earned them the most accolades up to now.

I jumped in on bass, hitting the strings a bit too hard and turning each note into a shattering "whomp." Too loud for sure, but it felt so right. I found a progression and began repeating, endlessly. I reached a mental plain, thinking that I could fall asleep right there and my fingers would keep going.

A few weeks after the failure of the big blonde experiment Walter paid Dr. Warren a visit, with a proposition. This was not a time to lick your wounds, Walter told the disgruntled principal. It was a good idea to teach the kids modern politics and history, but it was spoiled by a bushel of bad apples. It was a time to forge ahead and implement a bigger and better idea, rather than just retreat and follow the lesson plan."

Walter proposed a field trip to Washington, DC in late April-early May. The school would take a select group of students—no bad apples allowed— to the nation's capitol as a way to illustrate the civics lessons that had already put them to sleep. He would arrange a visit with the redoubtable Rep. Dan Kirkman, along with tours of the White House and the Capitol Building. Following this, the students would spend the weekend enjoying the culture and museums the city had to offer.

"It won't cost the district a dime," Walter said, heading off Warren's expected objection. I have a friend at the Better Government Education Project who can get

us a $5,000 grant. We need to use our own buses, but can raise the gas money by charging the kids on a sliding basis. We can charge Kirkman's kids $400 each and let the less affluent ones ride for free."

Warren liked the idea because it made sense, but also it stood a chance of rehabilitating his reputation. They started an application process, in search of 25 students who would benefit from the experience. The district had just purchased four new school buses, with one appropriated for the trip. With this in mind, the district took out all the seats to create a single surface where everyone could stretch out and relax.

The district should have known the trip wasn't going according to plan when Walter hired two students to paint peace patterns onto the bus.

It was never discussed one way or the other, but there was never any doubt that I'd go on the trip. We left on Sunday, with Walter, Mrs. Britting and 23 kids. Artie and Randy came along but Sparky decided to sit it out. Randy brought his guitar and a battery powered amp. Unexpectedly, he played lullabies and slow show tunes on the road, lulling us to sleep.

We were on the bus for two and a half days, arriving Tuesday morning. As soon as the Notch faded from view I heard a sharp, high-pitched ringing in my ears. The farther we traveled the louder it became, although it subsided when I got out of the bus and into the wet spring heat.

They pulled into a parking lot near the Jefferson Memorial, in a space that contained a dozen buses parked in a semi-circle. Walter parked in a way that almost closed the loop, and it was clear he knew our campmates. It was also clear that the money collected for a hotel would be saved and spent on something else.

The idea that we were to follow a schedule of tours and hikes was quickly tossed into the adjacent Tidal Basin. We were to use the bus encampment as a home *base, to come and go as we pleased. There were some touring options, the White House and the Capitol, but anyone who'd rather go to a museum or climb a monument was free to do so. Meals would be served at noon and 6 p.m. every day from the bus camp's communal kitchen, and we got $75 spending money to last us the week.*

I decided to take a walk, skipping the Capitol trip and the visit to Rep. Kirkman planned for that afternoon.

I sat at the edge of the Tidal Basin, cogitating a plan. A few minutes later a reedy black man with cysts that followed his jawline sat next to me and asked if I wanted to buy some hash. I always wanted to try the stuff, but remembered how in some places the drug dealers and the police work together. The dealers find a mark, sell the goods and then call the police who swoop in and make the arrest. The dealer gets his dope back, and the cycle begins again.

I was about to reconsider when he turned at me and hissed.

"Shit. You're a narc." He pushed me, but my center of gravity was low enough to prevent me from toppling into the water. He bolted, leaving a small paper bag. A few minutes later two policeman walked by, one black and one white. The white guy tipped his hat at me saying "nice day."

I waited a few minutes more and had a look inside the bag. It was full little cubes wrapped in tin foil, of varied shape and size. I popped them in my pocket since I had no way to smoke them.

I walked around the White House to 16th Street heading north, going up to V Street and turning right. Two blocks later I headed south. The world had changed and was now void of cheeriness. Many of the buildings were burnt out or boarded up. The street was sparsely populated, but unsettling nevertheless. I soon attributed this to being the only white person around.

I already knew about prejudice and racism, having lived through the great blonde experiment. I knew that racism was based on fear, but I wasn't particularly scared of the people on the street. Unlike the blonde thing, there was no principal telling them that it was OK for them to beat up white people that week. They didn't seem too worried about me either, so I felt safe enough.

That was until I got down to around P Street and heard a group of men screaming at each other and waving their fists. They were all black, and very scary although they did not notice me at all. Part of that was their being wrapped up in their argument, but it also had to do with my crossing the street as soon as I heard the chaos.

They were arguing about baseball, and whether it mattered at all if the Washington Senators moved to Texas.

The next day I walked toward Dupont Circle, which someone told me was the place to be, for the young and hip. Going up Connecticut Avenue I heard a rumbling bass voice from blocks away. As I got closer I saw a dapper black man with a pencil mustache and dressed in a dark suit holding a giant bouquet of multicolored balloons.

"Make the ladies happy, make the children happy," he brayed. "When the ladies are happy everyone's happy. They're big, they're beautiful." I was tempted, having a few of these around the bus camp would lighten things up, but I wasn't going to walk all the way back holding a bunch of balloons. Or even one.

I heard the routine about four times before drawing up next to him. I wanted to ask a question, to hear his story. Just when I was about to say something he looked me in the eye.

"They're big," he growled. "They're beautiful."

Walter had ranted on for years about equality. How blacks or greens or reds or whatever were as good (and *in some cases better) than everyone else. This was all abstract, as there was only an occasional black person visiting the Notch and none at all at school. After the blonde disaster, I knew a little more about prejudice, but nothing at all about its victims.*

I'd been here just a day and had already seen hundreds of black people, just walking the street on their way to somewhere. The ones I'd seen up close—rabid sports fans and a deranged balloon salesman—were both eccentric in ways that I'd never seen. I didn't think that I knew anything about black people as a group or a race, but I didn't feel threatened or even noticed.

I thought of the blondes washout and Dr. Warren, and that I would recommend the best way to learn about another race and the impact of prejudice is to spend a day in a town where you are in the minority.

I was on my own. While Walter showed the other kids the significant sights of social protest, I was in the Museum of American history staring at statues of overdressed First Ladies wondering what they looked like naked. And while Walter took everyone to the editorial office of an underground newspaper, I was sitting in the stony, cool National Portrait Gallery, gazing at oil-paintings of presidents and patriots.

DC had more people than I'd ever imagined. By Friday the crowds had gotten louder and stranger. Lots of longhairs, not your average Wheeler type but full blown freaks, with long ponytails and massive unruly beards. Many of them walked around barefoot, carrying signs. It turns out this weekend's itinerary included the MayDay demonstration against the Vietnam War. The government hadn't stopped the war so it was the demonstrators' goal to stop the government. After a weekend of festivities, the 40,000 protesters were going to take to the street and bring the government to a halt.

That Walter had scheduled our little field trip on this particular date was not a coincidence.

Saturday morning we had a little meeting. We each got another $50 and were told to meet back at the bus at noon Monday to prepare for the trip home. We were to observe but not necessarily participate in the efforts to shut down the government. If possible we should stand behind any professional looking photographer to cut the chances of appearing in a newspaper.

Randy asked me where I'd been, and whether I wanted to go to the afternoon concert with Artie and him. I said sure, but we'd meet up later. We decided to check back at the right of the stage (not "stage right") at the edge of the crowd. I took my little bag of hash and gave each of them one third of the booty.

Randy put his guitar on his back and said he'd see me later. I wondered if he expected to end up onstage at the free concert. I wasn't going to rule that out as it had already been a pretty strange week.

I began making my way toward West Potomac Park. It was was just across the Ohio Street bridge from the bus camp but I decided to take the long way around, through the mall. I'd never seen so many people in one place. I realized I hadn't eaten, and there was no food in sight, so I chewed down three pieces of hash. It tasted good, but a little greasy. So I had two more.

When the music started I began walking toward the sound. The sun was bright and the air thick and heavy. I was sweating, determining that DC was probably the only place that you could drown just walking down the street. I could see the air wash around my head.

It was another ten or fifteen minutes or two hours when I realized that everything had increased brightness and the damp air was visible in swirls around people and places. I kept walking toward the music, through a thickening crowd. The music sounded fresh, clean, and familiar. They sang about a "riot going on," which wasn't exactly true even though it fit the mood. Nothing needs to be exact or literal, here.

They played old surf songs, "California Girls" and "Wouldn't it Be Nice." Randy would go on tears where he would play two or three songs from the same band, so these guys were drawing on the Beach Boys. After a third Beach Boys song I realized these guys weren't imitators, but the Beach Boys themselves. Pushing close, I saw they all had scruffy beards and hippie clothes.

I never liked the Beach Boys. They were of another time and the surfing message always seemed a bit ridiculous. But today they were fresh, familiar, and intricate. The sun, the heat, their beards and the hash all melted together. The bliss was short lived. I started feeling a little claustrophobic during "Sloop John B," which finished with the line "this is the worst trip I've ever been on." It was then I realized that I wasn't actually standing up, I was held in place by the people next to me. I was smashed in the middle of a crowd. I was relieved that they were all seemingly happy, and not hostile. Which caused me to imagine them as hostile and know that I had to get out of there as soon as possible.

I pushed through the crowd toward the front edge of the stage, finding a grassy space big enough to lie down. I stretched out and closed my eyes. When the band kicked into "Good Vibrations" I opened them again, watching the clouds geometrically form and transform in time to the music.

It was their last song. When they stopped I started to sweat again. As if every note had a cool breeze attached. When they stopped the heat became oppressive.

After about twenty minutes—or forty minutes, or four hours, the music began again. It sounded good enough for a live show, but all lacked the majesty of the opening act. NRBQ's rock and roll sounded a bit out of sync,

People were craning their necks for a look at Linda Ronstadt, but all I saw was long legs and a bare midriff. I heard some other sounds at the edge of the crowd, then finding Randy and his little portable amp surrounded by about 30 people. He was doing a straight-out imitation of Jimi Hendrix, although the songs were not recognizable as Hendrix. He seemed to notice I was there, playing a few bars of "Spirit in the Sky" as acknowledgement.

There was a helicopter sound but the flying machines weren't visible. Balloons were everywhere, set adrift to confound the helicopters and prevent them from buzzing the crowd. In the distance I heard my balloon guy. "Make the hippies happy, make the happies hippy. Make the police unhappy. They're big, they're beautiful."

An announcer spoke with enough authority to quiet the crowd.

"Ladies and gentlemen, we are presenting to you one of the best musicians in the country—no, one of the best musicians in the world. Can you please welcome Mr. Charles Mingus."

Another voice kicked in.

"Nixon's been assassinated! Agnew's president! And he's declared war on Cuba."

"We're still here, anyway," another voice, perhaps one of the musicians, piped up.

They started playing, but it wasn't really music. It was slow and moody and didn't seem to go anywhere, or ever kick into a higher gear. I tried to slow myself down as the music peeked through, but it never took hold.

Nixon dead? Agnew president? I hoped Walter had nothing to do with this. And if he did, I wondered who would drive the bus back home.

I lost interest in the music so I decided to take a walk. Finding a copy of the Washington Post that someone had left on a bench, I imagined tomorrow's front page. A giant headline screaming "AGNEW!" atop a caricature of the vice president. The guy had a huge nose. I saw a line and got on the end, not knowing what it was for. Maybe I can get something to eat or drink. It turned out to be a pay phone. After about an hour—or a week or a year—I got to the beginning of the line. I inserted a dime and dialed the number printed in the paper.

"Newsroom." A woman who sounded a little like Lois.
"Hi. I'm at the demonstration. Has Nixon been shot?"
"I don't think so. Let me check."
I thought we were safe, or no more unsafe than yesterday.
"No, he's fine," she said. "Where did you hear this?"
"It was just going around. Maybe I heard it wrong. Thanks anyway."
"You're at the demonstration," she said, waking up a little. "What's it like? What's going on?"
"Crowded and hot," I said. "It takes an hour to make a phone call because of the lines. And the Beach Boys are way better than Charles Mingus."
"Oh, so you're not one of the political ones," she said. "Thanks for calling."
I hung up feeling stupid and that I'd wasted an hour, but wasn't sure what else I would have done that was any better. I started walking toward a new musical source. It sounded like Randy again, but he was not playing Hendrix anymore. It got louder as the air suddenly cooled, and I heard the riff that Randy used to signal the return to the verse after minutes—or hours, or days—of improvisation.

The monuments faded, and I was back in the ballroom with a bass in my hand pumping out six bars of A followed by a C to D transition. We tried to take it home but didn't stop at the same time.

"Outstanding," Randy said. "Lois will be here in a few days, and we're ready for her. That was great, Paul. I can tell you've really practiced."

November 13

I can play patterns endlessly and passionately if I am
the only person in the room. If I know, someone is
watching I freeze. This isn't acceptable behavior, for a
musician who can only reach their potential if no one is
listening. So I learned to deal with the phobia. I practiced
the song parts until they became muscle memory and
kicked into patterns during the improvisation. I turned my
back to the audience and just started playing. Once I
found the groove I essentially lost consciousness, until
Randy sent a signal—a harmonic or twisty note—that
brought us back to earth.

On yesterday's little voyage I re-lived one full week
of my personal history in about eight minutes. It was all
authentic, up to the time I heard Randy's guitar take over
the Washington Mall. I was grateful to not re-live the next
two days, when Walter, Mrs. Britting and every student
but me were arrested during a massive military operation
designed to shut down the demonstrations. Which it did
quite thoroughly—although it appeared that it was all a
big joke on the government.

Since I was the only one not in jail I needed to figure
out a way to spring them. I had to succeed, because there
was no way I would be able to drive the bus back home
by myself. This wasn't hard. When I went to the
courthouse to investigate there were lots of nice men who
agreed to get the class out of jail in return for paying a
small fine and signing up for a possible class action suit.

Last year the local paper did a story on me,
characterizing me as someone who had never left
Wheeler's Notch or Wheeler proper during my entire life.
There wasn't anything else going on at the time,
obviously. The reporter confirmed my theory, saying
"slow news day" as she shook my hand.

I felt playful, or pissy, and decided to not say
anything about my little DC sojourn. When looking back

at 15 you can never say what absolutely did or did not occur.

After ten years, it may not have happened at all. Here, I end up as a local curiosity, the man who never left town. I'll be 30 in two years, at that point it will be a milestone. At that point I'll be locked into the game.

"Gee, I'd really like to drive to Albuquerque to see the Kinks," I might say. "But I don't want to break the streak." I don't know whether there would be any backlash if I copped to the DC trip. I never actually said that I had never left town. Other people made this assertion, which I didn't take the time to correct.

I'm back on the Cricket, writing away. Artie cut back my hours, first saying that I only needed to stay by the phone from noon to 4 p.m., then telling me I didn't need to be there at all until further notice. Hundreds of machines were almost ready to go. There was a glitch in the operating system or, more specifically, disconnections with the Cricket's modifications of the operating system. Having the machine chirp instead of beep at startup worked only occasionally. It would alternately chirp, beep, or crash, with no apparent pattern. It had become so inconsistent that Microsoft threatened to pull our operating system licenses because of unauthorized changes to their code.

I don't really need to be here, but I've grown attached to this little green bug of a machine. The keyboard has a soft touch, but just enough play for comfort. The eight-inch monitor has a clear resolution, although all the letters are green. This nearly matches the computer's color, which is a pretty cool visual effect. If I turn the lights down, it feels like I'm writing through an infinite tunnel. Especially since the individual pages have no beginning or end.

My enthusiasm wasn't shared by the reviews editor at a major computer magazine who beat us up pretty hard about many little things. Artie sent me the review through an interoffice connection, which went a long way to explaining his snarly mood.

FRANKENCRICKET?

By Pete Winterschien
PC Eye Magazine

You can buy an IBM PC in any color, one salesman told me, as long as it's beige. This isn't a bad thing for now, at this stage of the game it makes more sense to offer technical competence and capability rather than giving people color swatches when they visit ComputerLand.

But there are some people who want something a bit snazzier looking for their home or office, and some companies that are lining up to fill that need. The first such effort comes from an outfit called Cricket Computer, which is located in the midwest. Silicon tumbleweeds anyone?

There are a few things to like about the Cricket, improvements that could be incorporated in future versions or by other companies. However, there is a lot not to like, beginning with its designated pale green color reminiscent of a squashed bug or a iridescent St. Patrick's Day outfit.

The biggest annoyance comes right out of the box, when you turn it on for the first time. Instead of the generic beep used by IBM, Compaq and all available compatibles it emits a metallic crickety noise. Anyone who has lived in the country knows what real crickets sound like; you can only imagine what it would sound like if someone decided to throw the annoying little insects onto a grill. That is to say, you don't have to imagine it anymore.

The cricket sound comes from two representations of the insect, a small one on the CPU and a second larger one at the top of the monitor. When the machine is booting up four insect eyes flash red, when it is ready to use the eyes all go green. This is presumably to keep people from issuing keyboard commands too soon, or to keep them amused during the comparatively long boot-up time.

In somebody's cute idea of what customers want, the cricket noise persists through the time the computer is operational. A choice on the startup disk allows you to set the chirp for a specific time, or have it just peep at random. Unfortunately there seems to be no toggle to turn it off altogether.

Aside from the green case the Cricket rearranges the standard CPU-monitor-keyboard equation. Instead of tethering it to a cord, the keyboard slides out of an adjustable drawer on the bottom of the CPU. There are five positions, from abutting the CPU to extending out two feet. It's strong enough to support itself, so you could put the machine on the edge of a table and the drawer would serve as a desk substitute (although you don't want to put any weight on it, and there is nowhere to put your coffee or cigarettes).

The keyboard is fair, with an action midway between the stiff click of the IBM and the mashed potato-like models on the Compaq.

The monitor slides into the top of the CPU, making an electrical connection that does not require a second power cord.

The most revolutionary aspect is the slide-out motherboard. You flip up the front of the PC as if it were a car hood, and the PC's innards come sliding out. This allows you to change expansion cards, check connections and dust inside. This is great, because as PCs become more popular users are learning how to install updates and expansion cards themselves. However, the relatively underpowered Cricket isn't a power user machine, so the people who are likely to do regular upgrades will want something with a bit more punch.

The machine has a standard 8088 processor, which is already a little behind the times. But the $999 machine doesn't nickel and dime us on needed features, it arrives with a full 640K RAM and a 1200-bps modem, both necessary items for which most manufacturers require a premium.

It has parallel and serial ports along with a connection for an external monitor (the Cricket monitor also has a video interface port). This could be interpreted as a nod toward flexibility when in fact it is a backup system. The slide-in interface doesn't always make a solid connection at first. Once you use it for a while, it could break down entirely; so this feature extends its logical life.

Another cool feature is the generous 10MB hard drive connected directly to the motherboard. In the unlikely event that you'll ever need more space this will be upgradeable, although you will need to buy the larger disks directly from Cricket due to a proprietary interface.

When people always ask me which PC they should buy I have two pieces of advice: Buy IBM, because they are the standard setters and you won't have compatibility problems. And buy the largest, fanciest, and most full-featured machine available, since everything is going to be obsolete before you know it.

But some people are looking for a lower price, and flash. What they are really asking me is how little can they spend and still be part of the PC revolution. For them, I say try to find an overstocked IBM PC or XT. Not the cheapest option, but the most stable.

I wouldn't suggest buying a Cricket. Despite some cool features it seems assembled from different parts, like a carpenter's head attached to a bricklayer's torso. They are close enough, but don't really work together that well.

If you are looking for flash along with a choice of cool colors, you can remove the computer case and paint it any shade you like. You can even spray paint on

*sparkles and texture. And it won't chirp at you while you
are on the phone with a client, or when you are online
late at night and don't want to wake up the family.*

*Cricket is taking the bold-or-foolish move of
marketing direct to customers by mail. You call them, add
accessories and slap down a credit card. It will arrive
within a week, at which time you call a company rep who
guides you through the setup. I can't tell you how good
that service is. I snapped the three parts together without
any instructions, and didn't find the call-in card until I
was finished with the setup. I'd be interested to see if this
is just as easy for a novice user, as I have a better
computer instinct than most people.*

*Maybe someday everyone will be as smart as me
about this, but I doubt it.*

"This is horrible," Artie said of the review. "I don't
know what I expected. I bought some advertising space
announcing the Cricket and the sales rep said that I might
be able to get a review in the same issue. I didn't think of
it as a quid pro quo, but didn't expect to be shafted like
this. I guess that computer journalism is a new vocation,
and they want to show they are as tough and objective as
regular news."

This was a real blow to our little company. Our cash
flow was negative as we weren't even on the market yet.
We'd already missed the COMDEX computer show,
which is going on right now in Las Vegas, because the
booth costs were so outrageous. But we should have gone
anyway, Artie said. He'd gone last year, and almost
everything on display never made it to market. It was all
about meeting people.

He suggested that we should take a last minute
chance. If we left in an hour and both drove straight
through we'd make it for the last day of the show. The
pickings were rich, he said, and we could surely find an
investor or distributor.

I told him that I'd rather dig up Mrs. Babian's bones. That wasn't enough of an argument so I appealed to a sense of logic.

"We'll get there strung out and needing a shower," I said. "And still, no one will want to go into business with us, looking like we do. I sure wouldn't."

November 15

We've been practicing as a threesome, taking it about as far as possible. Randy is an articulate guitarist, able to play lead and rhythm simultaneously. The notes often sound like the human voice filtered through a massive wall of static. I was never that great of a bass player so there wasn't that much to re-learn, but after a week of practicing I'm better than I ever was.

I've discovered the source of the extra sound, the resonance, but haven't said anything about this to Randy or Sparky. Aside from a "nice job" after we finish the song they've never acknowledged hearing or feeling anything different than the three of us.

Bass playing, for me, is all about repetition. When Randy and Sparky go off on their little tangents I provide a foundation, the musical sun around which those crazy planets revolve. I begin the pattern, sensing the chord changes through muscle memory and instinct.

So I focus on a spot on the wall away from any hangers on and slip into an unconscious state, returning when Randy sends out the harmonic that signals the improvisation's end. As soon as I slip into a dream the noise begins, a keening, crying melodic sound that bends shape in relation to the other instruments.

This has happened twice since we started practicing as a trio, It happened most recently when SMUG opened for the Future Star, who felt the resonance and wanted to capture it on record.

It has always come and gone on its own, with no particular pattern. We characterized it with a musical cliche, "getting in the groove," which is as good an explanation as any. Or it was, until I figured out that it only occurred when I slipped into a trance.

I'm not sure how to bring this up with the others, or even tell anyone at all. It can't be forced. If I let on, there's a chance that we all might try for the equivalent of inducing a musical coma. I'm pretty sure that won't work, in the same way that you can't pass out while other people are loudly imploring you to go to sleep.

The wisest path is to just keep it to myself and hope that I can slip into dreamland at least once during each show. Hopefully for the last or next to last song. No audience wants sensory overload early in the set, and it will make the rest of the show anticlimactic.

Since playing the bass is admittedly boring I slip out of consciousness a little bit at a time during every song. In this case, the degree of resonance corresponds to how far underneath I go. The true sound never manifests when I can hear it.

The dreams aren't always pleasant. They are usually true to life, replaying a scene I've already lived in detail. In the middle of a vision, I couldn't tell you whether it was real or not. During sleep, my dreams are always covered with a film that indicates whatever I do has no consequence.

Most of these relived memories are benign, like climbing the hills above the goat lady's house or shoveling the piles of snow that fill the hotel's driveway every winter. Lately there's been a dangerous light around the edge of the visions, where I need to stay clear to keep from falling in.

Yesterday, we were sketching out "Young Man's Fantasy," a new Randy song written for Lois. I wasn't sure she was going to like the concept of singing "I'm the young man's fantasy, I'm every guy's type" repeatedly, but the music was solid and we could always change the words. Although with Randy, his rough draft lyrics better fit the music than a subsequent rewrite.

We started playing and I slipped into a state pretty much immediately, reliving a day that I long denied existed. Because the truth is, I left town more than once.

This journey began when a guy named Bill came into the café one afternoon with six people that could only be musicians. Bill was road managing this group, known as The Planets. They had played in Wheeler the night before, and drove up to check out the Notch. They were booked at the hotel, before attempting the precarious drive down the west end of the mountain the next day.

It turned out that Bill and I were both huge Kinks fans. There really weren't many of us around, this was before they became arena rockers but well after they had made some of the greatest music ever. They were in a bit of a holding pattern, their last few albums were good enough but not really special. They were treading water.

Bill said they were touring and were playing in Albuquerque, where he lived, in about three weeks. I said this sounded great, but I never left the Notch unless I was going to Wheeler. He jotted down a date, September 9, and told me that if I came to the show he could get me in. I could even stay at his house, which was just east of Albuquerque. That's an eight-hour drive, I said. Worth it for the Kinks, he said.

After dinner and a few beers he invited me up to one of their rooms. They'd pushed the bed to the wall and created an open space with a semicircle of chairs facing a table with a Sony reel-to-reel tape deck. There were guitars and small amps all around. We continued drinking rum and smoking joints, which led to the inevitable musical hijinks.

Dave, the sound guy, was fiddling around with multiple tape speeds, complaining that the deck had only three options: 1 7/8 inches per second, the slowest, then 3 3/4 and 7 1/2. The faster the speed the better the sound.

After giggling for about an hour, we settled on a mission.

"What if we did a version of "Squeeze Box" by the Who as performed by Crosby, Stills, Nash and Young masquerading as the Chipmunks?" Dave asked.

I had to pinch my own hand, just to be sure I wasn't crazy. A slight pain, but the room didn't shift so I'd probably heard him correctly.

So we sketched out a routine. The song lasted for two minutes and forty-five seconds at normal speed, so we attempted to lengthen it by half. We'd play a take back and it would be too fast, so we needed to slow it down a lot more. We got it right, and decided to do a final take.

A few bars of an open G chord and verse one begins.

"MaaaaaaaMaaaaaaa's gohhhhhhhht aaaaaaaaa squeeeeeeeeeezeboxxxxxx sheeeeeeee wearrrrrrrs onnnnnnn herrrrrrr cheesssssssst……."

I played a slow pattern on G, D, and C. We did the bridge and then began the 12-bar instrumental break. Here, Dave and Bill kept the tempo but fired out notes as fast as they could. Final verse, then home free.

We sped it up to 7 1/2 ips and it still raced a little bit, but it was late and we'd had a shitload of pot and wine.

We then cut the opening gag. This was a little trickier. Bill's voice was supposed to sound normal while the responses—from me, Dave and Steve the drummer—were supposed to sound squeaky.

"Crosby?" Bill said.

"Here."

"Stills?

"Here."

"Nash?"
"Here."
"Young? Young!!!! YOUNG!!!!"
A pause and then a snort.
"OOOOOOOOH KAAAAAAAY!"
*Dave faded in the song at that point, the tinny
guitars, squeaky vocals and walking bass. The original
bass line was competent and precise, but its doubling of
speed made me sound flash. It still was a little too fast,
but it wasn't going anywhere. Before I fell down drunk
Dave cut me a cassette and Bill said something about
getting it on the radio in Albuquerque.*

*Bill left me with a bag of mushrooms, saying he was
saving them for the concert but if I brought them along he
wouldn't waste them on some other band. I told him that I
couldn't commit right now. He said think about it, you are
not going to have another opportunity like this.*

*I woke up before dawn on the concert date and hit the
road. I hadn't missed the fact that I hadn't been to a real
show since seeing the Future Star, and that was basically
on a work night.*

*I was driving a Datsun 620 I'd bought a few months
before when the VW died. I'd also brought a large plastic
tape deck, called a "ghetto blaster," that was tethered to
the cigarette lighter as I played Kinks and Stones tapes
all up the road.*

*My mood lifted in proximity to the mountains, so by
the time I reached Interstate 40 I was close enough to
cheerful. This part of the trip is astonishing, and coming
out of the mountains into Albuquerque from either
direction is a spectacular sight.*

*I stopped for lunch around 30 miles out and ate a few
mushrooms. My first mistake of the day.*

*I wasn't sure exactly where the show was. It was
somewhere on the University of New Mexico campus. Bill
had told me to call when I got to town, giving me the
number of the music store where he worked.*

I called from a phone booth in the student union and told that Bill wasn't in, that he was at home recovering from last night's Kinks concert. They changed it, I asked. No, it was always the 8th, I was told. Where can I find Bill? He's out in the mountains. If you come to the store I'll draw you a map.

The bad news was I had driven hours for nothing. Worse news, I started tripping.

I sat in a plush chair for two hours that turned out to be ten minutes, and decided to go somewhere else to ponder. I went into a place called Newsland across the street, one of those stories where people stay for hours reading magazines standing up. Except I was having trouble standing and the pages wouldn't focus.

I found the car and turned the key, managing the half mile to the music store by driving on Gold instead of Central. Lots of stop signs but less traffic.

Lorenzo, the manager, looked at me like I was really stupid. He drew me a rough map, saying I could either get on the interstate at the middle of town or right out Central Avenue all the way.

The eastward stretch of Central Avenue was an endless series of hotels and restaurants but I didn't want to get on the interstate until I really had to, it didn't feel safe.

I walked into Wild West Music, plunging from bright sunlight into a dusty darkness. There was a bank of guitars on one wall and on display racks on the sales floor. There were rows of amps and accessories. I blinked and walked to the sales desk where I saw someone who looked more like a Lorenzo than anybody there.

Everyone in the store had a messy beard. They were dressed in T-shirts, shorts and flippies, or wearing overalls with no shirt underneath. Every one of the customers was wrapped up in something; a guitar, a violin or a saxophone. No one paid me any attention and none of the sales staff (I counted four possibilities) asked if I needed help.

I walked up to the guy who looked most like a Lorenzo and told him I was looking for Bill.

"You Paul?" he asked.

"Yeah."

"You're the bass player on that 'Squeeze Box' thing,"

"Uh, yeah." That's why the cold shoulder. Bill had no doubt played the tape to his friends, laughing at how ridiculous the guy from the Notch was.

"Bass part was great," he said. "The rest was just stupid. I can't get away from it these days."

"You could just change the station, man," said a scruffy shirtless overall beard guy.

"They play it on KZZX every day on their morning show," Lorenzo said. "I have a five minute drive to work, and they always play it when I'm in the car. I left ten minutes earlier or ten minutes later. They always play it as soon as I leave the house."

"Sorry," I said.

"No, man, you didn't do anything. Bill bet us all he could get it on the radio. If he couldn't he'd work here for free for a month. If he succeeded I give him a PA head. So it was pretty high stakes, on both sides."

I started getting really antsy. I had to leave immediately and started walking toward the door.

"So, man, don't you want directions to Bill's house?" Lorenzo said.

He told me to take the Tijeras exit, go under the highway and head on the service road six miles until I saw a rooster mailbox on the left. Bill lived in a small cottage out back. I'd call him to say you're coming, but he doesn't have a phone, Lorenzo said.

The road I took was a dead end so I had to go on 40 another exit. This one corresponded to the map, which had no indication about how steep it was.

I drove to the top and pulled into a small turnaround. The car barely made it up the hill. I looked down the other side to see a stream running over the road before it all went up again.

So I made the day's first smart move, just a few freeway exits from where I'd made the dumb one. I turned around and headed back down the hill.

I had been running all day, toward something that was at first uncertain before disappearing and leaving me in a hostile town cold and tripping. What I didn't need is to get stuck in a river with no real destination and no money. Add that I really didn't want to see Bill. especially since I wasn't exactly sure why I was there in the first place.

The bottom of the hill led to only one path, to head east toward home. Going back to Albuquerque didn't make any sense. Might as well go home and cut my losses. Maybe I could find a half-decent meal as soon as I felt like eating.

Which ended up as a Wendy's 180 miles away. I was tired of looking so I grabbed the low hanging burger, as it was, and got home at 3:30 a.m. In a parallel universe, where I make better decisions I'd be hanging out with the Kinks.

This day was a complete fucking waste. I drove 600 miles and didn't get anywhere. I had a destination but no purpose. Which is why I never told anybody about this little adventure. I'd forgotten it completely, until Randy's new song dislodged the memory.

The day wasn't without benefit. My first psychedelic experience was hash-induced at the May Day March and my last was on this maritime drive. In between I did psychedelics another eight-or-so times. But it was this day that I realized how frightening these experiences were, and why I will never trip again.

"Young Man's Fantasy" closed with a bang, ending my own fantasy in its wake. Andy came into the ballroom holding several sheets of black paper. They had arrived in the mail, individually addressed to Sparky, Randy and myself.

Glancing down, we saw the same cut out letters spelling out threatening messages. "SMUG should go." "Leave SMUG be."

"Stop Playing Now."

"This is creepy," Randy said. "But at least they're not saying we have to die anymore."

November 16

Randy called a special practice today at noon. Lois was here, good news because we've gone about as far as possible as a trio.

I hadn't been in the same room with her since SMUG broke up, although I had seen her pictures in magazines and on the first Anita album cover. She had lost weight since graduation, which was the opposite of myself and most of the people I know.

While her general appearance had changed in ten years her public appearance changed more frequently. Her hair was straight, cut in bangs while shoulder length on the sides and back. It was straight, fine, and usually black, although she'd gone platinum a few times. She often dressed in a glittery jumpsuit, one that wasn't particularly revealing but accentuated her grace.

Randy and Sparky arrived just before noon in the blue bus, but Lois was tardy. Sparky and I headed to the ballroom while Randy stopped to talk to a woman who was seated in the café. She was small and unassuming, with bangs and a mop of frizzy hair tied back. The bangs tipped me off.

Lois had arrived the night before and checked into the hotel without letting anyone know (her parents still lived in Wheeler). She smiled at me when I recognized her, neither hostile or particularly warm.

She was carrying two cases, each with a Hagstrom guitar. One was the old familiar yellow while the second was a bright shiny blue.

"These guitars are outliers," she said. "But they still have the best action and the best sound. I got the blue one used in New York, because old yellow won't last forever."

We started with "Peace Time," a new Randy song. Lois jumped right in, coming in on cue on a song where I'd never heard the words. Which Lois sang without a lyric sheet. Either she was very good at observation and improvisation, or Randy had sent her the new songs in advance.

We ran through it twice, as was our process, then stopped to talk. I learned that Randy had sent Lois one of Artie's rehearsal tapes along with a set of lyrics, which she had memorized.

We did six more, pretty much all that we had practiced. We easily pulled together a 75-minute set. Add "Cloud Pictures" and "Spirit in the Sky" and we could play an actual concert tonight.

We stopped at around 5:30 and went into the café for dinner. Sparky and I sat on one side of the booth with Lois and Randy on the other. I sensed a stronger connection between them while we were playing. This was confirmed by their behavior now. They sat close together and were always touching each other as they talked.

"So when did this happen?" I asked. "I didn't have a clue."

"We've been talking for a while, and I went up to New York last week to get her down here. I didn't tell you because you're disinterested in the band and seem to want to get out of it as soon as possible. So I wasn't going to bore you with the details."

I felt left out. I had been consciously pulling away from the band, but I was expecting Randy to pull me right back in. I didn't want to commit myself to the band but didn't want to end the experiment just yet.

Randy had changed the rules. I expected it would be a push-pull thing for a while, after which I'd relent a little bit and agree to stay on a while longer. Now, when I said I wanted out soon he acquiesced immediately.

I had previously agreed to play the reunion show and nothing after that. He had taken this to heart, making subsequent plans that he did not share.

So I went for a walk.

Outside, I pondered. If he was manipulating me, I wasn't going to give in just yet. They'll need me for the show, so we have about a month before any decisions need to be made. I couldn't count on that either, maybe he's already made plans for the band that don't include me.

I've never wanted to be especially engaged with what's around me, or even what is supposedly happening in my own life. I just want to live here comfortably, day to day, with no interruptions or diversions. This is a challenge, people want me to get involved in different plans and schemes, and my energy is spent on avoiding those responsibilities.

Playing music has snapped me out of this. Each day I can't wait to start playing with Randy and Sparky, really paying attention to the fingerings and the changes. It's not just patterns anymore, but long fills and little finger tricks. I love the "whomp" the E-BO makes each time I hit a note. I'm especially psyched about Lois completing the puzzle.

The biggest obstacle right now is overcoming stage fright, which still scares the shit out of me. The strategies of turning my back or pushing myself into a trance work well enough, but I don't yet trust my ability to play at full potential while unconscious.

I came back inside. They were still there. Lois and Randy were snuggling while Sparky stared off into space playing a distracted rhythm with his bare hands.

I tapped the table.

"Tomorrow at noon," Randy said, without breaking the snuggle.

November 17

I tried to sleep late today, but there was a huge ruckus outside of the hotel. I came down to the café, where Andy brought my coffee and told me what all the noise was about.

"One of the sheriff's deputies parked his cruiser near the overlook last night and went off to see his girlfriend," he said. "When he came back this morning, the car had disappeared. They didn't have to look that far, it turned out someone released the brake and pushed it over the cliff."

The initial noisy panic resulted from the idea that someone had driven the car over, but a look through the binoculars determined the "driver" was one of those crash dummies, so the panic level decreased for a few minutes.

That was until the deputy fully realized his predicament. He was supposed to be on Notch night duty, the most boring detail in the county. There is no crime up here, and the town follows the disappearing practice of never locking their doors.

Or that's the party line. We always lock up all the outdoor cabins, and anyone who has moved to the Notch during the past five years doesn't feel bound to that tradition. They lock up at night and even during the day sometimes. This has a lot to do with how some long term residents treat newcomers, not exactly threatening but not welcoming either.

The deputy was tall and skinny with a shaved head. He reminded me of the greasers in high school, which wasn't a surprise. I recognized him as Eric Steel, David's older brother who spent much of his time tormenting the undergraduates after David was turned into a goat and had to abandon his post.

Eric's anger originated from a loss of property and disrespect for the law, but was exacerbated by the fact that he'd sloughed off for the night to get himself satisfied.

"I asked him where he was, and I thought he would hit me," Artie said. "He won't say who he was visiting. Maybe she's married, or maybe she's 'he.' Either way, I wouldn't want to be in his uniform when he calls the sheriff for a ride down the hill."

Steel was outside, pacing and smoking. He came into the to use the phone, and his posture changed.

"Yes sir. I'll ask around again to determine if anyone saw anything. Yes, sir. No sir, I don't feel comfortable divulging that at the present time. Is it worth my job? I can't say, sir."

He hung up, then straightened himself up to his full height. He walked outside and yelled at a passerby. "Hey! You! I need to ask you a question."

Steel was angry and humiliated. It was only the second time in history that a sheriff's car was vandalized. Years ago Granger, the current sheriff had pulled the same maneuver that Steel did last night. The car wasn't pushed over the cliff, rather it was beaten several times with some kind of pickax. All the windows were broken, and the tires were flat.

Fifteen years have passed since I became "Hamster" and felt the full power of the bullies' wrath. I was living in fear and could never go to The Pizza Palace because it was the creep hangout. "But I don't really like pizza," I would say, having never eaten anything but the frozen kind.

One of the reasons I don't like going to Wheeler is that I would often see an ethereal version of David Steel lurking around and ready to pounce. This was never real, as he was never seen after christening me as a rodent.

In recent years, we've heard that he is living in DC and working for the government. He's probably on Reagan's environmental team dismantling all the rules or the USDA working toward officially designating ketchup and relish as vegetables.

I haven't imagined David's presence for some time, so it was disturbing seeing lookalike Eric in a uniform. The sixties and seventies brought us hope, growth and change. Here in the eighties, evil has assumed the driver's seat.

I looked up to see Randy, Lois, and Sparky get out of the blue bus and nearly run into Steel. He was talking loudly, while they were first nodding and shaking their heads. Randy said something that looked like "we stayed in Wheeler last night and didn't see anything."

Steel appeared to turn toward Sparky who shook his head. This didn't seem to be appropriate as Steel was looking for a verbal response. But, the more he asked the questions the more Sparky just shook his head.

We tuned up but didn't start playing right away. Lois, who was elated last night after practice was now in a dark mood.

"Everything's falling apart in New York," she said. "I told them up front I wouldn't be back until December 20th, and they signed off on it. Now, they're all worried about the album and the tour and want me back right away.

"The rest of the band wants to practice over the holiday but we don't need it right now. Everything's nearly perfect, all we need is a one week refresh right before the tour."

The tense situation worsened when Lois pointed out that she hadn't played with SMUG for ten years, and they made up for lost ground in a single evening. She had said that playing with SMUG was exhilarating, the first indication that the sojourn was more than a one-off obligation.

"Fuck them, I'm here to recharge myself," she said. "Let's go."

The first rehearsal sounded better than we expected but we were paying too much attention to what we were playing. Today we loosened up some. Lois became animated, trying some of the moves she'd learned in New York. By the third run-through it had become a performance, with Randy and Lois interacting with each other like Jagger and Richards or Bowie and Ronson.

This threw off the balance we had before, when Sparky and Randy went wild as Lois and I provided the anchor. Now, it felt like I was the sun, around which three crazy planets followed a fractured orbit.

We wound down at around 6:30. There were bright lights outside, coming from a large winch that was dragging the patrol car over the top of the cliff. The crash dummy was still in the driver's seat. It had a menacing, painted-on grin, and a shaved head. It was wearing a thigh-length leather jacket. A key was in the ignition.

For the second time that day I thought of David Steel, and felt a tinge of fear. I pulled myself out of it, the same way you eject yourself out of a nuclear nightmare.

November 18

I knew Ronald Reagan was president, that my mother Denise Collins was a U.S. Representative from upstate New York and that Dan Kirkman Sr. is still our congressional representative. I know the names of our two senators and the governor, but can't tell you the names of our county commissioners or anyone else on the local level.

I know that Tom Granger is the sheriff because he was here over the weekend investigating the stolen police cruiser. And I know that Beverly Reilly is the mayor of

Wheeler, because she was just here to discuss plans for the Wheeler Centennial, in which SMUG will take part.

Mrs. Reilly is about 5'2" and slender, with a short haircut. She wore a polka-dot shirt, black jeans and cowboy boots. I imagined that she was about two inches shorter without them.

She said it was uncertain exactly when Silas Wheeler came to town, guessing it was in the early 1890s. The precise founding date of the Notch was also in doubt, as the original population was a band of artists who didn't really care what year it was. 1984 was an arbitrary time for the centennial, since it fell more or less in the middle of those two events. December 15 was also arbitrary. She admitted that choice was a bit odd, since the middle of winter wasn't the best time to schedule an event that included a series of outdoor activities.

"I think it will be quite a festival," she said. "Wheeler has never thrived like other western towns because it really isn't on the way to anywhere. It was built from the perseverance and motivation of those who saw this area as a slice of heaven. It has never been easy to live here, but is well worth the effort."

She was practicing her speech, which needed a little work but might sound good in front of a crowd of those whose ancestors persevered.

I decided to help her off the soapbox and asked her what SMUG's place would be in the celebration. She said that we would be asked to participate in the parade on Saturday December 15 banquet, atop a float that was designed to look like a bandstand. We would not play but would wave to the crowd while we wear our instruments. Lois would not have a guitar because she was something of a national celebrity, and we didn't want to spoil the visual.

I said that Lois was a bit uncomfortable performing without her instrument. Which was something of an issue in her new band. When she was with SMUG she never performed without her trademark Hagstrom. But since the rest of the festival was historically nebulous I would see what I could do.

After the parade, we were to be honored at an evening banquet to include many of the notables who had called Wheeler their home. This included Rep. Kirkman and his sons who were being groomed as his successors. There would be room for both, as census redistricting in 1990 was expected to slit the single district into two.

She asked whether I could persuade my mother to appear, as she gained some notoriety during her senatorial campaign. I told her that Denise would probably rather chop off her foot than set it in Wheeler or the Notch.

"We can discuss that later," she said. "Perhaps we could persuade Artie Connors to appear, as his Cricket Computer is at the forefront of the technology revolution."

That might not be too wise, I said, since it appeared that he was closer to the forefront of bankruptcy.

I asked what other celebrities might appear. She said that she was in touch with the owners of Wheeler's department store in New York but they were so far unwilling as Silas Wheeler was something of a family renegade who was banished to the footnote pages of the family genealogy.

Anybody else, I asked. Not that I can tell you, she answered.

After the banquet SMUG would be asked to play for 20 minutes. We would be asked to leave the Marshall stacks home and use smaller Fender amps and the county PA instead of our own equipment. We should play "Cloud Pictures" first followed by "Pretending" and use the remaining time for a song of our choice. "I hear you like to improvise," she said.

I told her we were rehearsing a 90 minute show and that the Fender amps could barely compete with Sparky's drums. Lois was spending a month down here to prepare, at some inconvenience. We had never opened with "Cloud Pictures," and never played "Pretending" at all as it was a throwaway track.

After each exchange her pasted on smile lost some wattage. At this point she couldn't hide her irritation.

"You're so negative," she said, before shifting back into mayor mode.

"We appreciate your participation and your contributions to Wheeler's legacy," she said. "We regret if it causes any disruption to your daily lives but remember this is a community event.

"If you feel that your little rock band deserves more attention perhaps you should sponsor your own function. We can make it part of the program, as long as it isn't on December 15."

Her smile returned, and we shook hands.

Randy, Lois and Sparky arrived an hour later. They weren't happy about Mrs. Reilly's edicts. Lois wondered why she had come here for a whole month. Her protest was perfunctory considering her rekindled relationship with Randy.

Sparky nodded and said "whatever." It came out as a nasal whine, a clue to why he never spoke.

No one felt much like practicing. We could have gone to the banquet cold and played three songs, as all this rehearsing was unnecessary under the circumstances.

To cheer everyone, and myself up I took up Mrs. Reilly's suggestion.

"I know my obligation is for one show only, but this is insane," I said. "Let's put on a show the night before, on December 14. We can play a full two hours if we want. It would have nothing to do with the Wheeler Centennial, which seems to be a made-up thing anyway."

My little pep talk worked. We picked up the gear and pounded out an energized version of "Cloud Pictures" out of the gate.

A new Randy song, "Get Offa Me." This one's chugging and repetitive. It began with a bass riff out of "My Sharona" and layered on the sound until it sounded like "I Am the Walrus." The chorus called on Lois to bellow "get offa me, I've had enuffa you."

The ballroom was empty which was a good thing, because this is not the kind of song you play in public. Randy was offering up a big "fuck you." We didn't have to play what we were told and had the opportunity to let all of this energy loose. "Get Offa Me" could make it into the show, but I was rooting against it at this point.

I was looking out of the lodge window about a week after Steel had come up with Hamster. It was snowing, and Deputy Granger's car was parked across the street. It was all well lit, so I could see a large brown goat with a single horn walk toward the sheriff's car and start kicking. It drove its mono-horn through all the windows. It did not bleed. It jumped up onto the truck of the car, then the roof. Stomping as he went. He jumped into the snow and looked me directly in the eye. This was unnerving because all the inside lights were off, and there should be no way he could see me.

He had a single craggy horn in the middle of his head and a pile of pus where the other should have been. There was a curvy 's' on his forehead. He was drooling and appeared to be laughing. I sneezed, when I looked back out he had disappeared. Thirty seconds later there was a crash, as he knocked down my bedroom door.

Except it wasn't a crash. Sparky was slamming his cymbals to get my attention. We didn't have much of a smooth landing here.

"Paul is telling us that he doesn't like this song much," Randy said.

"I don't either," Lois said. "These words are fucking sick."

I struggled a bit, reluctant to say what was on my mind. But what the fuck.

"I have a question," I said. "Does anyone know what happened to Mrs. Babian's goats? You know, the Goat Lady. She died, maybe ten years ago."

Randy, Lois and Sparky were clueless, but Artie piped up from behind the reel-to-reel.

Her daughter sold the land to Eric Steel who hauled in a pretty nice double wide. He left the shack, and I'm guessing the goats are still there."

"Including his brother?"

"That was never proven. You want to try that song again?"

"Not really."

November 21

After abruptly leaving town nearly four years ago Walter is returning. Tomorrow. For Thanksgiving.

Andy told me the news this morning, with a happy bounce in his voice. I have no idea how he and Walter connect romantically anymore, but they are each other's best friend. And Andy misses his friend.

He told me that tomorrow wasn't going to be a huge deal, just something pulled together for staff and their families. He gave me kind of a weird wink when he said that, so maybe he was planning something bigger. I couldn't tell for sure. He had an odd facial tic so a wink could be easily misconstrued.

We've practiced every other night or so. There was no pressure, it's a whole month until the show. And I don't know if I'd really call it practicing because we rarely stopped during a song for correction or discussion. We never played the same song twice. We were getting comfortable and familiar. Remarkably, I began practicing on my own. Everyone was encouraging and supportive.

It crossed into another level of bliss when after one particularly inspired version of "Cloud Pictures" Sparky piped up.

"Yeah."

I can't speak for Randy, but this was the first time that Lois or I ever heard Sparky say anything.

Practice today was a little unsettling. Randy and Sparky arrived with about 15 friends, coming up the hill in the blue bus. I wasn't prepared for this. Over the past few days I worried if having people in the room while we're playing would break the magic. We didn't discuss this before playing. To address it would lead to a discussion, and at this point we'd rather play than talk.

It was a bit of hard work. I couldn't connect with the songs, playing just a little out of phase. I was aware of the shapeless people in the room who seemed to grow in number. I wasn't having fun, and the audience must sense this. Which means they weren't having any fun either. These stressy feelings made it impossible to slip into another plane and I was unable to lose consciousness of the situation.

I slipped into these little trances quite frequently, which meant that I didn't ever hear the band at its peak. It was like being robbed, to be most proficient on my instrument when I had no idea that I was even playing.

Randy and Lois are doing their little romantic thing, huddling on stage for twenty minutes before we started up. I wasn't listening, but it was clear their conversation was half planning their dual guitar attack and the other half figuring out what they were going to do when Lois had to return to New York and become "Anita" again.

We played a full set, and I was able to ignore the hangers-on. We'd gone for about two hours before kicking into the closer, a slowed-down version of Dylan's "Maggie's Farm." Audience or not, this was probably the best we've ever played.

When I walked into the café it was clear that Andy
was understating the "something pulled together for the
staff and families" part of his Thanksgiving plans. The
was transformed, with a the service counter turned into a
buffet. The regular dining tables were removed , in their
stead picnic tables set end to end and covered with what
appeared to be a continuous white tablecloth.

There was turkey, ham, prime rib and duck. The
expected trimmings; mashed garlic potatoes, sweet
potatoes, stuffing, squash, beans and a few unexpected
ones—corn, brussels sprouts and a huge fruit salad.
There were special orders, like the canned asparagus-
hard boiled eggs—cheese and pimentos in a white sauce
that Martin from maintenance couldn't do without.

We always practiced in the ballroom, but our
equipment was set up on a portable stage in the hotel
lobby. Everything was ready to go, we were obviously the
after-dinner entertainment. I had somehow missed the
notice that we were supposed to play today, in front of
people. Making a fuss about this seemed churlish. I didn't
want to do anything that would spoil the party.

I tend to fade back in big crowds, just observing. If
people look my way or approach me they'll think I'm
aloof. The truth is, I have trouble enough knowing what
to say in the first place. It's even harder to know what to
shout.

I got a beer and sat at a back table, but I wasn't alone
for long. Artie found me and sat down.

"Wow, this is spectacular," he said. "Andy didn't
hold anything back, and all for Walter."

I told Artie that I wasn't holding my breath, that I
would believe it when he actually arrived.

"He's right over there," Artie said. "Although he's
changed some."

Sure enough. He was nearly unrecognizable, with
hair clipped above his ears and a neat goatee. He was
dressed in new blue jeans, a wrinkled white shirt and a

*blue blazer. No tie. Ruby was the formal one, she sat at
his feet looking up, wearing a clip-on bowtie.*

*He was talking to a woman with short red hair, whom
I recognized right away. Anita. Maybe I can get my pin
back.*

*"What's his story?" I asked Artie. "He seems like
he's calmed down some."*

*"That is the one and only Wally Trout, the computer
king," Artie answered. "He owns 30 stores up and down
the west coast, and is a big fucking deal. He only sells the
products he likes, and he provides full support for those
products, indefinitely. He's brought humanity and
compassion to the computer business. They aren't just
machines, he says, but our new way of life. Our friends.
He's really quite innovative."*

*"And he could sell the Cricket, giving us a some
exposure," I know where this was going. "That is if he
likes the product."*

*"Yeah, that's the next step," he said. "I need to get
him alone and give him a demo. Is everything working?
And presentable?"*

*"Sure, but this is Thanksgiving, family time," I said.
"Maybe we should wait until tomorrow."*

*"No, he's actually leaving tomorrow morning for a
retreat in New Mexico," Artie said. "I don't think it's an
issue, since these big computer people never stop
working. That's the great part about technology. It doesn't
make you take time off if you'd rather get something
done. Your ideas don't stop coming at 5 p.m., so you can
always find a way to express creativity and help your
business. Around the clock."*

*I didn't know if he was implying that we should cast
off the shackles of the workday and offer 24 hour tech
support. I wondered if this would cut into band
rehearsals. Maybe after all these years I was going to
learn how to tell Artie no.*

"Oh, look he's stopped talking to that squirmy little redhead," Artie said. "I'm going to go introduce myself. Re-introduce myself."

Lois and Randy sat down as soon as Artie left. They were cuddling, or whatever new couples do. I switched to vodka soda.

"Hey," Randy said. "Did you talk to your old man yet? He seems like he's changed some."

"That's what I hear," I said. "I'll catch up with him later."

In alternating voices, they told me about plans for the band. The SMUG rehearsals had revitalized Lois and reawakened Randy, to where they were playing better than ever before. While Anita-the-band had a bright future, now was the time to take decisive musical action.

Their plan: Randy and Sparky would join Anita-the-band, as a second guitarist and second drummer. Lois would ditch the guitar to become lead singer. I would get to stay home and quit the band, keeping the promise that I only needed to play one show. Randy was excited about this part, since it allowed him to keep a promise of which he planned to renege. I acted as if it were a good idea, what I always wanted, but secretly felt a little sad that the music adventure was going to end.

"I think this will work," Lois said. "People might need to get used to the idea of two drummers, although a lot of bands have them today. Two bass players, um, no."

Anita walked by and Lois leapt up, introducing herself as someone from high school that Anita probably wouldn't remember. Which Anita didn't.

"I'm a singer now," Lois said, understating. "I would watch the cheerleaders practice, and was awed by your grace and coordination. You were an inspiration to me, and I named my band after you."

"What, you named it 'Realtor?'" Anita said, somewhat unkindly.

"No, we're called 'Anita,'" Lois said, stammering. "We are putting our second album out soon and will be opening for Dire Straits on a tour next year."

"That's nice," Anita said, reaching into her jacket pocket and pulling out a card. "Send me a copy. Also if you ever want to come back to Wheeler to live I can put you in something nice for way less what it would cost anywhere else. Of course, you'd need to live here, but nothing's ever perfect."

Anita looked at me, then right through me. I didn't smile, only acting like someone who lost something valuable a long time ago and wanted it back now.

"Good seeing you, Paul," she said. "I still have your pin. If you stop by the office I can return it to you. Have you ever thought of selling this old behemoth? I'm sure it would be quite popular as mountaintop condominiums."

Randy and Lois moved on, and were replaced by a tall guy with a shaved head, wearing a suit.

"Hello, Paul," he said, in a mannered voice. "My name is David Steel."

"Um, hi," I said. "I thought we turned you into a goat." Not what happened, but I was a bit flustered. He laughed, and slapped me on the back.

"I was troubled when I lived here and wasn't very nice to you," he said. "I was a bit of a bully and was perhaps obnoxious and destructive."

Um, yeah.

"What's your job now?" I said, maybe a bit too angrily. "Are you an underestimator, or something?"

Accept and survive and forgive, they said. But this creep named me after a rodent, and all I wanted to do was gnaw off his fingers.

He laughed again.

"No, I'm a mathematician for the the United States Bureau of Standards in Gaithersburg, Maryland," he said. "I haven't come back to Wheeler since I was yanked out of school for being an asshole. I'm glad it happened

*before blonde week because I really might have hurt
somebody."*

*He apologized for sticking me with this stupid name,
saying that he had "issues." I wasn't going to let him
slide on this, so I just nodded when he got up.*

*A short guy in an elf suit, complete with the curlicue
slippers, sat across from me. Since I'd only met him once
it took a minute to recognize Bill from Albuquerque.*

*"I owe you an apology, man," he said. "I wasn't
really sure whether I told you the right date for the Kinks
show, but you didn't sound like you were going to make
the trip. I should have called, I know, but it escaped me."*

Yeah, I know. Those pesky details.

*"You should have seen that show," he said. "I've
seen them fifteen times and this was by far the best time.
At the end of the show Dave Davies took off his guitar
and handed it to me and then pulled it away. I thought he
was going to give it to me but obviously I read it wrong.
Still, I 'owned' that big fat Les Paul for a few seconds."*

*He said the most exciting part didn't happen at the
show but a few hours earlier, when drummer Mick Avory
visited the music store.*

*"We had him sign a drum head, but Lorenzo took it
home," he said.*

*"Too bad," I said. "We could have put it up here in
the café."*

*Bill laughed and pulled out a pouch of gooey brown
stuff. He ate a portion and handed it to me.*

"Mushrooms. Yum."

"No thanks, I'm waiting for the turkey."

*He laughed as I looked over at Walter. When I turned
my head back he'd disappeared.*

*So who's next? Dan and Jack Kirkman? Dr. Warren?
The past is gone for a reason, and these people should get
out of my head.*

*Instead, it was a woman with strawberry blonde hair
turning gray, appearing as a younger and more ethereal*

Mrs. Babian. Considering everything else, her return from the dead as a younger person didn't seem all that farfetched.

"Hello, Paul," she said. "I'm Denise Collins."

My mother.

"Um, yeah, it's nice to meet you." I leaned toward her, initiating a hug. She responded by squeezing, hard.

"I wasn't going to ever come back, I didn't think I'd ever come back," she said. "But I was driving across the country to decompress from the election and something drew me here. I really didn't expect this, though. This is really spectacular."

I asked if she'd talked to Walter. They had spoken, she said, and he seemed quite different. He was more directed and focused. He looked her in the eye and made her feel as if she were the only person in the world. Which is what started this whole thing for her, way long ago.

"I can't believe he really left the Notch," she said. I wrote you that I might have stayed with him if he had any ambition, or inclination to move away and find something new. He did that and it helped him greatly. I think we'll be friends again but don't expect anything more. I know kids often want to see their separated parents get together again."

Some "kids" probably do, I thought. But I'd never met Denise before and Walter never was "Dad" to begin with.

I didn't know what to say to her, so I went for the obvious.

"Losing that election must have been hard," I said. "It was so close and you were expecting to win. I was expecting you to win. I've always wanted a mother in the US Senate." I was flailing, now.

"Yeah, the House isn't quite as cool," she said, a bit crisply. "All I did was listen to constituent complaints, but spent some time outside Reagan's tent pissing in."

That was about to change, she said. The day after the election Reagan called her personally, commiserated with her about her loss and offered her a position as an FCC commissioner. Reagan said that he respected her commitment, even though she was a bit of a pain in the ass. He wanted some political balance on a board that would determine how to accommodate new communication devices and technologies.

"He really is a charmer," Denise said of the president. "I've hated him for years, his smarminess, but when he turns his attention to you it's hard to resist. He really seems sincere."

Walter, with Ruby in tow, sat down right then. "Of course I'm sincere," he said, patting her on the hand. "Not you," she said, pulling away. "Reagan."

"We disagree on this, obviously," he said, then looking at me. "You look familiar."

I smiled, nervously but also with a sense of relief. Walter wouldn't always acknowledge my presence in a real way, I was glad to see this wasn't going to change.

"This is really spectacular," Walter said. That word again. Did everyone leave the house today carrying the same adjectives?

Walter began talking to me, as if Denise weren't there.

"I've done some really stupid things in my life but it's nice to finally find the groove," he said. "I should have never had anything to do with your mother. Or maybe I should have married her. I shouldn't have taken on the management of this creaking edifice, or I never should have left. I always felt trapped by all this here, and what other people wanted of me. Which is why I became such a dilettante. I've always believed in individuals, in real people, so I've spent my time focusing on them directly. I didn't really care about the big picture."

He pulled out a pack of cigarettes, shook one out and lit it up.

"This new venture, technology, will change the world," he said. "A lot of products, like your friend Archie's little froggy computer, really miss the point. But it's a start. I'm going to start selling his machines in my stores, even though they are pretty lame. But they will draw people in, at which time I can sell them what they actually need, a computer that doesn't croak."

Walter didn't know he'd made a mistake, he really thought that "Archie" was pitching a computer that emulated a frog. Maybe he doesn't listen that well after all.

"Growing up here, I never wanted to leave," he said. "Although I resented the pull of this place. There's everything I ever wanted, right here. There were lots of challenges running the hotel, and never the same day twice. But now I'm getting to see the world, or at least California. My life was here for a long time, but I doubt I'll ever come back again."

Let Walter be Walter.

"I know you're comfortable here, and that your experience away was really terrible," he said to me. "But if you ever feel that you want to grow, to change. I can offer you any number of jobs in my stores. I don't think you'd be much of a salesman, but I remember that you like fixing things. The amount of things to fix in this world extends just about to infinity."

He dropped a card on the table. These things were mounting up as Artie had neglected to take Anita's with him.

Walter stood up and extended his arm to Denise, but she shied him away and said that she'd talk to him later.

"I wasn't entirely honest with you when I wrote that letter," she said. "There are some things that you should know."

She had written me about the last time that she saw Walter. She had made as if she was going to stay the night and even gone to sleep for a short time in Walter's bed as

I was in a crib nearby. The missing piece was the presence of another baby, my twin sister.

"That was why I was so pissed off at Walter," she said. "Cutting holes in the condoms was bad enough, but the fact that I ended up with two babies to raise was infuriating. Not that he wouldn't have helped, but knowing him it was certain that I was going to be in charge."

Walter was slack jawed that day when Denise brought over two babies. He knew of the pregnancy and wanted to help, making it clear that he wanted to be part of his child's life. Denise wouldn't have any of it. She told him firmly that she did not want to see or hear from him until the babies were born.

"There is a time during every pregnancy when a woman hates the father, because he is the one responsible for all the pain," she said. "If he hadn't put that little stick inside of her she wouldn't be miserable. Most women get over it, because they love their husband and want a family. I did neither, so I spent seven months being pissed off at him. It helped me get my mind off my own stupidity, that I needed to postpone my academic trajectory to sit on a mountain with a mother I hardly new."

To understate, Denise wasn't exactly tuned in to the whole family thing.

The babies were only a few weeks old, but their personalities had already emerged. I had a placid nature, I rarely cried and was happy just sitting in the corner. I would amuse myself with anything that was on hand and didn't seem to want a whole lot more.

My sister, on the other hand, was loud and demanding. She took 30 minutes to get to sleep, crying and screaming the whole time. When we were in the crib together she'd grab whatever I was playing with and make it her own. I'd find something else which she would immediately take away. And so on.

Denise said the difference was clear. Temperamentally, I suited Denise's easygoing nature while my sister was restless to the extreme. Just like Walter.

Her intent, that night, was to lull Walter into a sense of security, making him think they were going to become a big happy family. She would then pick up and leave, taking the (easygoing) me and leaving Walter with my (obstreperous) sister.

I asked if this sister of mine had a name. Denise said it was Petra. Petra and Paul. How adorable.

Denise hoped to show Walter the contrast between the two children, realizing his plight once finding he was stuck with the obnoxious one. Except once we settled into the crib we both achieved a docile state, playing quietly with each other, and sharing.

Walter and Denise had dinner, drinks and went to bed. Denise got up in the middle of the night and went to the crib, differentiating Petra and me by the hats we were wearing. Imaginatively, mine was blue and hers was pink.

Except we had switched hats when we were playing. Denise picked up Petra thinking it was me, wrapping her up in a blanket and taking her to the car. She set the child into a backseat travel crib and turned on the engine.

Hell broke loose. Petra began screaming uncontrollably, and Denise realized that she had absconded with the wrong kid. She also realized there was no turning back, and that she wasn't going back inside to attempt a switch.

Denise said she raised Petra on her own until remarrying when the little girl was three years old. Her husband loved her deeply, but Petra's inquisitive energy drove him nuts. They split up and the process repeated. After the second divorce Denise decided to continue on her own.

Petra turned out to be an art prodigy, gaining a spot in the Rhode Island School of Design when she was just

14. She became well known in the art world (as "PetraZ") for her fractured collages and surrealistic paintings.

"You look at a lot of modern art and think it's just finger painting," Denise said. "But Petra has a gift for realism, so her paintings never look sloppy or ill-conceived."

I said that I don't know much about art but I know what I like. I didn't say that from the description I didn't think that I'd like Petra's art all that much.

It was an unusual twist that over the past few months my past had connected me to three overachieving women; Lois, Petra and Denise.

Where is my sister now, I asked Denise. Right over there at the top of the stairs, she replied.

On the most basic level I never wanted to be a woman. There was not a moment in my life that I wanted to switch genders. Mostly because I'm happy to be where I am, but also because I'd be a pretty ugly girl. I was pleased to see that Petra was undeniably attractive, looking nothing like me in a wig and a dress.

I saw Denise's point, as Petra was a live conversational wire, waving her hands around and fixing her gaze directly on Randy, who was had a rapt expression and the inability to get a word in.

"Does she know who I am?"

"Yes, she of course wants to meet you but we didn't want you to be blindsided. Do you need a minute?"

"No, I'll go up there now."

I stood as the room began to revolve. I'd been drinking for a while and it hit me all at once. I couldn't walk but if I sat down again I might never get up.

The band started to play. My band. I didn't know that we were starting this early. I hadn't eaten. They—we—were playing "Maggie's Farm," which was supposed to be the closing number. Did they replace me and not say anything? I know that was about to happen but didn't think it was going to be immediate. Wasn't the reunion supposed to be the farewell show? I could hear the bass, which sounded great. Maybe it was good that I was going to step aside, even through I wasn't still sure it was what I really wanted.

"That was spectacular," Artie said, stopping the reel to reel with a snap. I heard clapping and whistling from somewhere behind me. An audience. It was nighttime, and all the food and decorations were gone.

"Okay, we may as well take the rest of the week off," Randy said. "We've come a long way and don't want to over-rehearse this. Let's have Thanksgiving with our families and start up again in next Wednesday or Thursday. We need to stay spontaneous."

Everybody left. I sat on a chair with the bass across my knee. I had a lot of these little trips before, going off in my head during an improvisation and visiting various places in my past. They were all authentic, I was reliving parts of my life as they happened. Tonight was the first time I moved into a different sphere, living an instance that had yet to occur.

I didn't know what was going to happen tomorrow for real, but I resolved to get some food before everything got really strange. The ideas that Walter and Denise had rekindled their relationship and that Randy and Sparky were joining Anita-the-band and that I had a sister seemed too weird to be true. Maybe they weren't, which was reassuring. Although I am not thrilled about living through the same day twice.

November 22

There was another ruckus earlier this morning. Randy, who had stayed in one of the guest rooms with Lois, began yelling that she was gone. The French doors were open, with footprints in the snow leading toward the ledge. He followed the footprints and ended up at the old cable car terminal. Except the cable line was broken and the car was nowhere in sight.

We called the Wheeler County Sheriff who began tracing the line from the bottom. They got about a mile up when they came to a crevasse, and it appeared that the giant red cable car was at its bottom.

Randy was distraught, blaming himself for going to sleep too soon. "She was really worried about what to do next," he blathered. "SMUG's sounded so great lately that she wanted to merge it with her New York band. She wanted me and Sparky to go there after the reunion gig. I maybe wasn't quite as pumped about the idea as I should have been. All I said was that I probably have to work at the lumber yard through the Christmas season."

"Oh, yeah, you should know that we didn't count on you coming to New York because you said you wanted to quit the band. And you can't really have two bass players."

That's twice I had to hear about this, and twice reminded that I was getting into this and didn't want it to stop.

Sheriff Tom Granger brought his chastised deputy, Mark Steel.

"I know you," I said.

"Yeah, I was a few grades ahead of you," he said. "You knew my little brother David."

Shit. Really?

"I know he gave you some trouble. I'd apologize for him, but the fact was you were a smarmy little runt who was walking around with a 'bully me' sign on your ass."

Who, me?

"There was this rumor that the creepy mountain witch turned him into a goat," Steel said. "Fact was, we yanked him out of Wheeler and sent his sorry ass to military school."

Granger called him away so I didn't have a chance to ask where David was today and whether I needed to watch my back.

As for Lois, there was nothing we could do. Pretty soon everyone walked the edge of the overlook with binoculars. Maybe she got thrown out and landed in the snow somewhere. We asked Randy what she was wearing. He told us it was a red sweat suit that was more fashion than warmth. At least we would be able to spot the body.

We went inside at around 1 p.m. Thanksgiving smells were everywhere. Andy had spiffed up the tables with white tablecloths and seasonal centerpieces. The food was all on a long buffet table, covered by a snot guard.

There was turkey and ham along with mashed garlic potatoes, sweet potatoes, stuffing, squash, and pumpkin pie. There was also a generous bowl of Martin-from-maintenance's special order; canned asparagus-hard boiled eggs—cheese and pimentos in a white sauce.

Walter and I spotted each other at the same time. He put down his plate and gave me a hug. "Hello son," he said. "It's really good to see you."

He was dressed in dirty jeans; heavy boots and a down vest. His hair was tied back and his beard was scraggly. There was a dull film of sweat on his face and his nails were black.

"You don't look so great," I said. "You want to wash up? No one's in your old room, that I know about."

"Yeah, in a bit," he said. "Right now I'm starved." He looked around the room, where everyone was looking at him curiously.

"Maybe I'll clean up now," he said. "I look a little shabby, and these folks haven't seen me in a while."

He walked off listlessly. Ruby followed, her stubbed tail in a slow wag. Usually Walter was all over the map, articulating random ideas and pithy observations, with Ruby hanging on his every word. Now, they just acted defeated. You can call him random or flaky but he was always awake, alive, and enthusiastic. Right now, he was just a slug.

The biggest difference I found when he returned was that he lost his focus. His greatest talent was always paying attention to others as they spoke, making them feel as if they were the only people in the world. Now, as he told me what he'd been doing for the past few years, he didn't look me in the eye at all. His eyes darted back and forth, as he ate as if someone would snatch the food away at any second.

He had a feral, wounded look. I remembered seeing a version of the same expression about ten years ago, when someone forgot to turn on the oven and there was no turkey for the 2 p.m. meal. That same someone decided to postpone all the trimmings, and the finished turkeys came out of the oven and were placed on the kitchen's cutting board at around 7. At that point everyone descended on them like vultures. Walter was in the middle of it, but his wild, feral expression had a joyful backdrop.

We had plans for about a dozen people, but the bad weather and the search for Lois cut it back. A scattering of staff and friends dotted the redecorated café, while Walter, Andy, and myself sat at a table in the corner.

Walter told us he had spent the last few years exploring the west, as a kitchen refugee. He'd find a town, searching for a with a "help wanted" sign in the window. He'd apply, providing a fictitious back story like his home was destroyed in a fire or his wife had left him for another woman and taken the kids.

He'd do anything, dishwasher, waiter, cook or cashier. His growing up in the had taught him all those skills to where they resided in muscle memory. He'd find a place to live, and kept to himself. After a few months, he'd move on to the next place.

He drove a Ford van he could sleep in comfortably, so it could be weeks before he landed elsewhere. He kept to himself, politely avoiding friendships and connections. To the people who saw him he was just a guy with a dog in a van. Not something you'd notice.

He came home because he was tired and deflated. He needed to feel part of his past and do some repairs on the Ford, but he expected to go back on the road in a few weeks.

I needed to be the adult here.

"Obviously, you can stay here as long as you want," I said. "Your name is still on the deed, and you haven't been declared dead. As for restaurant work, we have a little place here that can always use the help."

"I might like that," he said. "When I worked here, as an owner, my heart was in the place. So every up or down affected me. Out on the road, I wasn't responsible for managing anything, and I saw things that could be improved but didn't have the power to do so. I miss that."

We weren't serving the public today, although anyone who walked in would be invited to dinner. We were taking the day off as far as being a restaurant goes. Martin from maintenance had drawn a sign on a small blackboard but the chalk broke, and it read "Closed for Thaksgiving."

Walter saw the sign and didn't react, which was way out of character. A few years ago we were in a part of Wheeler we'd never visited and passed a store with "Custom Floor's" in raised letters across the top of the building.

He parked illegally and stormed into the store, demanding to talk to the owner. There was a lecture about misplaced apostrophes, the difference between possessives and plurals and the fact that such a mistake perpetuated bad usage and would contribute to the decline of knowledge.

"Oh, gee, I've never noticed that before," a saleswoman said.

"My point, exactly," Walter said.

In the following months, Walter went out of his way to drive past the store, parking illegally and running into the store to harangue the staff. It was irritating for them and embarrassing for me whenever I was tagging along. I would usually wait in the car.

Years later we drove by and were greeted by a large "Closing" sign in the window. The one, Ben, was on a fireman's ladder taking the grammatically challenged letters down. Walter started climbing up the ladder, demanding ownership of the errant apostrophe. Ben was too shocked to argue and handed it over.

"I'm putting it in a glass case where it can do no further harm," he said gleefully. That didn't happen. We got home, and we set in on the chair but Ruby, then a puppy, chewed it to bits.

That Walter didn't react to "Thaksgiving" was evidence that he was now a shadow of his former self

"Reagan has taken the life out of me," he said of our newly re-elected president. "When he was elected I knew he would disassemble all our recent progressive changes. I felt hopeless and was going to leave the country and go to Canada or Mexico. Instead, I ended up in places like New Mexico and Oregon. Both are slow enough and remote enough to seem like another country."

He said that Reagan had moved toward destroying the environment and was in big business' pocket. His initial Secretary of the Interior and Environmental Protection Agency appointments, both now gone, had shown a lack of respect for natural resources. And the idea of trickle down economics, where tax cuts for corporations create jobs for the working class, is a sadistic, misguided doctrine.

"Right after Reagan's first election was the last time I talked to your mother," he said. "She was more upset than I was about the situation, if that's possible. She said she would fight him in congress. Her goal was to make sure that none of his legislation is passed. She told me that she had stormed into House Speaker Tip O'Neill's office and called Reagan, among other things, 'a cheerleader for selfishness.' O'Neill used the phrase without giving Denise credit, which pissed her off. No compromising for her."

I wondered how Walter would react to the news that Denise was to become a Reagan appointee for the FCC Commission before remembering that I had imagined it during yesterday's particularly invigorating SMUG rehearsal.

We finished eating and moved to the lobby. Walter pulled a rectangular white thing out of his bag that looked vaguely like a piano keyboard except the keys were little black and white buttons. He began playing some melancholy notes that followed no particular tune. He added some percussion, and then sampled his voice saying "hello." The single word was stretched out and compressed on each note. These were mournful, expressive sounds that the manufacturer did not intend.

"You can't get these anymore, they are more than five years old," he said. "But you don't need a fancier model for what I want to do, to carry it around and take it out when I hear a melody in my head.

"It's a harmonica for the 1980s."

He fiddled with a few of the buttons and began playing something that resembled "Danny Boy." The sound was that of a metallic flute, as if it were played through a storm drain. It left "Danny Boy" and morphed into something else. No one else was in the lobby, so it echoed through the room.

The sun reflected on the snow outside, and the notes sent me to another place, almost as if I were playing bass and wanted to tune out the people around me. I noticed the little unit had an output jack and wondered if we could work it into SMUG's act. Walter really needed a new gig, although I could imagine the audience wondering who the old guy was and what he was supposed to contribute.

November 23

Mark Steel was waiting for me when I came down for breakfast, saying that he had a few questions. We sat at my regular table, and he pulled out a notebook.

"When was the last time you saw Miss Hannah?" he said. Right to the point. No reminiscing or asking how David was doing or if he were going to appear and cause trouble.

"Last night, after we finished playing we had a bite to eat. She went to her room with Ran—Mr. Powell around 9:30. I went out for a walk."

"Where did you go? Did anyone see you"

"On the path behind the lodge, and no. Am I a suspect here?"

"How was she acting? Was she depressed or drunk?"

"No, and no. We had played a phenomenal rehearsal set and were all pumped up. She said something about leaving her band in New York and hooking up with us again, but I think it was just the adrenaline."

I told him that we playing as SMUG for a reunion date next month. I said that he may have remembered us, because we had sort of a hit record about ten years ago.

"I was in Vietnam at the time and never heard it," he said. "My little brother wrote me about it and said it was a piece of shit."

Delayed reaction, he hadn't acknowledged my "am I a suspect?" query. This was now a hostile situation, but I knew I hadn't done anything to hurt Lois and had nothing to do with her disappearance.

"I never did anything to your 'little' brother," I said. "He used to torture me, gave me a stupid nickname and disappeared. Where is he now, anyway?"

"In the hospital. He's had a few mental issues. Even with that, he's twice as smart in his sleep than you are on your best day."

This was veering away from the idea of an objective investigation.

"I don't know what you have against me, but I had nothing to do with this," I said. "Perhaps I should talk to another officer."

"You've lived here all your life," he said. "You know damn well how small our department is. You want to talk to someone else? I can walk you down to the jail and wait until someone is available."

No need to get nasty. Ah, too late.

"How do you feel about this little band of yours getting together again? I heard you really didn't want to participate."

"I really didn't at first. Now I'm on the fence, but I think it might not be my choice. I don't want to go on tour or make a record or anything."

"Right. Being a rock star is a painful existence. I would much rather be a local sheriff's deputy or a hotel manager."

I waited. He opened a legal envelope and pulled out a sheaf of black construction paper.

"We acquired these. 'SMUG Must Die.' 'Keep SMUG Dead.' 'The world does not need SMUG.' 'Keep the past in the past.' There are a few more. Do you know who sent these?"

"You 'acquired' some of these from me, so no, I don't know who sent them. I find them disturbing, and now that you bring it up it's one of the reasons I'm not entirely chuffed about starting this up again. They shoot musicians, you know."

"I've heard you play bass," he said. "You're not really a musician, you're a dilettante."

I turned it around. "Are you sure you wouldn't rather interrogate someone you don't hate?"

He lost the leer and spoke quietly.

"Look, you're right," he said. "I don't really like you, and I need to be more objective. It's a small town. There aren't many officers and not many suspects so we're stuck with each other."

That was a joke. I think.

He asked whether we could talk, just as two people. I said sure.

He told me that David, his little brother, was sensitive and socially awkward. He was smarter than everyone but didn't know how to relate so he lashed out at people. In high school, we could identify either with the hippies or the greasers. Steel said that David wanted to be friends with the hippies, my little group, but we had rebuffed him. So he became a greaser, to lash out against those who hurt him.

This had a certain truth, as I knew the five of us, SMUG and Archie, could be cliquish and cruel. I questioned the assertion that David had only two choices, because he could have hung out with the academic crowd. Either way, the first time I remember meeting him he had a shaved head and a hard fist.

Steel switched back from the caring older brother to the interrogator.

"Have you ever seen this paper before?"

"Yeah, it looks a bit like the stuff in the art room that we use to store supplies for kids who stay here. There's some black paper, but most of it is red and yellow and colors you can draw on."

We spoke simultaneously. He asked "when were you last in there?" as I said "I haven't been in that room for at least a year."

He asked whether he could have look. I found the keys, and we walked up to a second floor supply room. Everything was in place, aside from the space where the black paper should have been.

"I'll need to take this for fingerprints," he said. "I just attended a seminar with the state police, and they gave me a little kit."

He sat down at a table and pulled something from his bag.

"I'm going to need to take your prints for a comparison," he said. I sat down and went through the process, although we ruined the first card because we used too much ink.

"Just so you know, I'm pretty sure my prints are on that paper since I maintain the art supplies," I said, trying to wipe off my fingers with some toilet paper.

I walked downstairs with my hands widened at my sides as I didn't want to touch the white walls or the bannisters. There was no advantage to having everyone know what my fingerprints looked like.

"I'll be back tomorrow or the next day with the results," he said. "Don't leave town."

I wondered if that meant I couldn't leave the Notch and ride down to Wheeler, but since I hadn't done that it six months it wasn't an issue.

November 24

We were supposed to meet this morning to talk about next steps and how long we should wait before canceling the reunion performance. Randy called and said he was too upset to talk about anything. Since Sparky never talked it was just Artie and myself.

He told me that Cricket Computer was pretty much dead. He managed to sell the Wheeler Mountain House at a profit, which meant that he almost broke even for the entire venture once he sold the company assets. Needlessly, he told me that my first month's salary would also be my last.

I could keep the computer, and could keep writing. If there were anything left around here to write about.

"First thing, I gotta tell you, Wednesday night's tape is phenomenal," he said. "I sound balanced a bit and cut the chatter, coming up with something we could release as a double album tomorrow. We could really do this. Lois' record company called and said they'd be interested, especially since this whole disappearance thing has gotten them a tremendous amount of publicity."

Artie wasn't happy with the record company's attitude. There seemed to be two options for them, depending on whether Lois turned up or was confirmed dead. Either way there would be an increase in record sales, as *Anita: Name* had already re-entered the charts.

There was a third option, should Lois neither reappear alive or dead. There would be an air of mystery that would itself move record sales.

"I couldn't believe this lady," he said of the label exec. "She immediately launched into this marketing rap and offered me $100,000 for the tape. She lays out all these options, and not once asked about how the search was going. I was going to say something like 'oh, by the way there's been no progress,' but wanted to see whether she would bring it up herself."

Artie said the members of Anita-the-band were "pretty broken up" about Lois' disappearance but were also champing at the bit to either start rehearsal with Lois or work it out so someone else can take the vocals.

"I guess if there's a chance you might make it in the music business you won't let a little thing like the possible death of a lead singer get in the way," he said. "It's up to you, but I don't want to release this to capitalize on her misfortune. If she's actually gone we can make it a private pressing, a collector's item. If it's a mystery I don't mind capitalizing on that."

Unspoken was the option of finding Lois alive, in which case the decision to release would be hers and hers alone.

As for the reunion show, we were ready to play and wouldn't have needed any more rehearsal if it weren't for the emotional maelstrom that surrounded Lois' disappearance. Even if she came back. I wasn't sure if this would permanently throw us off, causing us to lose the musical rapport we'd developed in the last few days.

"Let's give it a week," Artie said. "If she's not back by then, we pull the plug."

November 25

The world was spinning so quickly I hadn't yet pondered Wednesday night's rehearsal, which was our best performance ever. Artie left me with a cassette which I listened to twice last night. I could see his point, how it was as good as many of the records coming out today. Mostly because it was lacking those cheesy-sounding processed keyboards.

There was something missing, but maybe it was just because a tape of the event can never be as exciting as actually being there.

I thought about the performance, remembering a discussion I had with a couple of guys I'd never seen before named Mike and Peter. Mike had fine blonde hair while Peter wore a wool hat.

"I think it's great that you don't use keyboards," Mike said. "Although I thought I heard them playing during 'Maggie's Farm.' It was a subtle organ sound that backdropped the song and gave it this moody feel."

"Shit, man, it was nothing like an organ," Peter said. "It was more like a wail, or an echo. It was just there, as atmosphere, but when I noticed it and tried to pin it down it disappeared."

"I've only heard something like this once before," Mike said. "In the old shower at my parent's house. I'd go in there, get, really high and turn up the hot water. The pipes would sing to me. There were alternating tones and voices. Kind of like tonight."

"Yeah," I said. "Whenever someone tells me they've heard this they are really fucked up on something."

I told them that I'd heard that before, how people heard a fifth sound even though there were only four instruments.

"We call it 'resonance,' because that seems to explain it best," I said. "I've never heard it though."

I told them of my stage fright, and my attempt to deal by blocking everything out around me. How when I put myself into this state my playing became automatic and actually more skillful than when I was thinking about the music too much.

I told them that I would lose consciousness during these times and be completely unaware of the music and my surroundings. Pictures taken during those times showed a completely impassive face, although my eyes were always wide open.

"He never even blinks," Randy said from behind me.

"How do you know?" I said. "You are always in a trance of your own."

Randy put his guitar into the case.

"I'm only vaguely aware of the sound, so it is real," he said. "The audience can hear it a lot better, or so I'm told. One thing, it doesn't seem to happen unless Paul is in one of his fugue states. I don't know how to control that, and I certainly don't know how we'd ever get it on tape."

Recalling that brought me back today and made me realize what I thought was missing. Mike and Peter were so adamant about hearing the wail during "Maggie's Farm." It wasn't anywhere on the tape. Drugs could be a variable, but I was really high last night when I listened to the tape. Maybe it was a special spirit, like an otherworldly being that casts no reflection.

My pondering ended with a blast from the intercom, as Walter told me that Deputy Steel requested my presence.

After meeting him twice and watching his little freakout about his stolen car I realized he had two expressions: Intense aggression and a rictus leer that masqueraded as a smile. Which is how he greeted me today.

"Good morning Mr. Trout, how are you?" he said. No answer given, and none expected.

"I just have a few more questions. We've matched your fingerprints to that on several sheets of the black construction paper, as well as some of the threatening messages. Can you tell me exactly when you may have touched this?"

I told him that it had been about a year. He responded that a new test proved that the prints were just a few weeks old.

"Technology doesn't lie, I guess," I said. "I've been in the supply room within the last ten days or so but don't remember touching the art supplies. Although if you say so it must be true."

Steel missed the sarcasm.

"So you admit it then. Why did you handle the black construction paper? Was it to make signs that would scare your bandmates away from going ahead with the reunion?"

"You're ignoring the fact that I got a few of these messages too," I said. "Which could explain why my prints were on the messages in the first place."

"I think not," he said. "You have been acting very suspiciously."

He said we weren't getting anywhere with this line of questioning, so he shifted.

"What were the last words you said to Lois Hannah on the evening of November 21?"

"I'm sure it was to tell her 'nice show,' or something lame. I remember teasing her about playing two identical guitars. In New York, you weren't really cool if you had only one guitar. I told her that two of the same guitar didn't make her cool, it made her a dork."

"How did she respond to that? Did she feel threatened? Was this a threat of any kind?"

Respect for the law. Respect for the law. Respect for the law.

"Not at all. The Hagstrom sound fits perfectly into SMUG and has the best neck I've ever played. I thought of buying a Hagstrom bass, but I love the EB-O and a bass player only needs one instrument to be cool."

"Let's agree to disagree on that. One more thing. Where were you on the night of November 16 and the morning of November 17?"

I looked puzzled until he clarified, Friday and Saturday.

"I went to sleep right after practice and first woke up around 8:00 to some godawful yelling. If I'm not mistaken, you were wondering where your cruiser was."

"Did you have anything to do with the disappearance of that cruiser? Were you involved in pushing it over the cliff with a dummy that looked exactly like my little brother inside? Why would you try to implicate my little brother in this?"

"I confess. I created a David Steel doll, even though touching such a monstrosity would fill me with abject terror. I opened the car with my duplicate key, stuffed in the dummy and leveraged his foot on the accelerator. I then turned on the car and threw it into drive. Do I get a trial or go straight to jail and not collect $200?"

So much for respect for the law, respect for the law, and respect for the law.

"Don't be an asshole," he said. "I'm just doing my job. Don't you ever watch any cop shows? I'm completely within my rights asking these questions."

"No disrespect meant," I said. "I tend to get sarcastic sometimes. If I can be of any help please let me know."

November 28

Walter and I spent a few hours together today. It was the first time we had an extended serious discussion as adults. Or ever at all.

I hadn't seen him for a few days and again didn't recognize him at first. He was clean-shaven with the first traces of a new mustache. His hair was trimmed, and he was wearing a plaid shirt and crisp jeans. His hands were clean and the nails cut neatly.

He sat down at my booth. Ruby jumped up next to him and stared at me expectantly.

"Don't worry about her," he said. "She's just not sure where you fit in. She's probably not sure where she fits in either."

Where, then, do we fit in?

"I have some ideas that I wanted to share," he began. "The place looks good but could be a whole lot better with a few changes. I think the needs a makeover, and a menu change. It does a good enough job with the eggs and grits crowd, but we can add some options. We don't have to get fancy or trendy, but we can make it a bit more interesting."

He had learned how to cook some new things during his adventures and had even unearthed a recipe for gourmet chicken fried steak. Considering the 's history this could be quite a draw.

After renovating the café, he wanted to redo the lobby and the ballroom. The floor plan and the furnishing wouldn't change much, but new materials would enhance the old design and meet in the middle, at "rustic."

"There are a few old Washington State that are about 100 years old and look exactly how they did when they were built," he said. "But all the wood in the hull and on the decks have been replaced with newer versions of the original material. They look classic, but the only original piece is the ship's bell and the wheel."

Not all of the wood would need replacement here, as the floors were still in good shape. Just cleaning and refinishing would restore it to a classic sheen.

Since Walter took over for the first time in 1966 the rooms were used sporadically. Half of them were opened to guests as needed, but they weren't deep cleaned or renovated. The bed frames, now antiques, were in good shape but new mattresses were needed all around.

For the first time ever, he wanted all 60 rooms to be open and ready. He wanted to promote the hotel as a destination, and even picked out a new name: Wheeler's Lodge on the Notch. I told him that sounded odd. He didn't take offense and said we could figure that out later.

The outside needed the most repair. We needed a new roof, and the stone walls needed sandblasting and pressure washing. Taken together, the place would look exactly as it did in Arnold Wheeler's imagination, before a series of events prevented it from reaching his potential.

The cost, he said, could be as much as $1 million. That, he said, was the easy part.

Two years ago he had a rare upscale job at a Seattle hotel when Arnold Wheeler III was a guest. Arnie had come to town to investigate a west coast version of Wheeler's department store but decided that it would be too difficult to compete with the established Nordstrom chain.

After a depressing dinner with his potential partners when the plan was scuttled Arnie had retired to the bar alone to ponder his losses. Walter, who had finished in the kitchen for the evening, took over at the bar. After a few drinks, Walter introduced himself as Arnie's half uncle.

"Here's the story," Walter said. "Your grandfather and his brother had competing mountain houses in the west as you probably know. Your grandfather spent half the year at his hotel where my mother was the manager. He got her pregnant, and your grandmother found out and made an ultimatum, that he was never to go west again. My mother married another man with the hopes of raising me, but when he found out about your grandfather he split."

Imagine the CEO of a department store chain ending up in a random bar in a strange town where the bartender pretends to be a relative while casting aspersions on the morals of his grandfather. Your average CEO would leave immediately, without tipping.

Instead, Arnie took another sip of scotch and nodded his head.

"So you are the 'other one,'" he said, smiling.

It turned out that Walter was something of a legend in the New York Wheeler family. Little Arnie, when he misbehaved, was always threatened with deportation to the west in care of his evil second grandmother and her gnome-like son. He was told that the evil grandmother was a slightly more attractive version of the wicked witch in *The Wizard of Oz*.

The threats had the opposite effect on Arnie. Instead of fearing them, he wanted to visit these people. When he was carving out a place in the corporation he fantasized about expanding in the west, taking over the Wheeler Mountain House properties and expanding into the hotel business.

By that time, neither property was still owned by a family member. And it was probably not a good idea to go into business with the wicked grandmother and the gnome son.

Arnie told Walter that his trip to Seattle descended from these expansion fantasies, that he never stopped wanting to expand beyond the overcrowded and unfriendly east coast.

Walter told Arnie that he may return to Wheeler some day, perhaps in a year or two, and would contact Arnie should an expansion opportunity exist. This was unlikely in the short term, as Walter wanted to tool around the country for another year or so and the property was now controlled by his own gnome-like son.

Walter promised to call Arnie if things changed, which he did yesterday. Arnie, still depressed by his expansion misfires, wanted to jump right in. The two hammered out a renovation plan. Arnie would hire out a crew and the whole process would take a little more than a year.

The details needed work, and legal input. The ownership of the hotel would not change, but the renovation costs would be paid off by the hotel's profits over a 30-year period.

Walter said he liked the idea but still needed to clear it with me. I'm not sure if there was a gnome reference here.

The ownership of the hotel isn't really specific, only deeded to "Hazel Earnshaw and her descendants." In that sense, Walter and I are equal co-owners. The matter has never come up, although the owner has always been the person who arranges to pay the property taxes.

I said I had no objection to moving forward. Walter told me that life as I know it would change drastically. The next year would be disrupted by construction, followed by a steady stream of guests and tourists.

Finally, the rustic edifice that provided a slice of local color would be transformed into a first-rate mountain lodge.

I still had no objection. Life as I know it had gone about as far as it could go. SMUG was probably dead, and I had no desire to play bass anywhere else. I'd spent my whole life avoiding the outer world. All of a sudden I wanted to see what was out there.

"There are a few other issues," Walter said. "As you may have heard, Wheeler County wants to build the road from the Notch down the west side of the mountain. Arnie also likes that idea and told me he could help get the highway funding. But I think it's best if it remains the way it is, a rocky path that is passable only to the brave and the foolish."

That was it for now. Our lives were over, but would soon begin again. Most people went out into the world in their teens or twenties. By the time they're my age they are completely disillusioned and ready for real adulthood. I never went out into the world and skipped straight into the disillusionment phase. Now I would get to see whether there was anything I'd missed.

Walter got up and shook my hand.

"Thank you Paul."

"Thanks Dad," I said.

I sat there for a minute. I couldn't remember ever calling Walter the D-word. Wondering whether it would become a habit I began drumming triplets on the table with my left hand, the G-B-D note pattern. I went a little faster, adding A, C, E, F# and back to G. Faster yet. I wondered if the tapping would prompt anyone to investigate. I didn't want that so I softened my touch. It faded into silence.

I assumed that Ruby left along with Walter (there, I knew it wouldn't stick. But she was still sitting in the opposite chair. She looked at me quizzically, cocked her head, got up on her hind legs and crossed her front paws.

"I have no idea what that means," I said.

She cocked her head in the other direction and recrossed her paws.

"You know that your father really loves you."

I didn't see her lips move. Do dogs have lips?

"He'd talk about you all the time. I got a little sick of it, actually."

"What did he say?" I blurted out without thinking.

"That it's generational for your family to lie to their children. His mother lying to him about who his father

141

was, and then he lied to you about your mother. He wanted to break the cycle, but he didn't know how."

"He could have just tried talking like a normal.....wait a minute, I'm not talking to a dog. Especially not one that used words like 'generational.'"

"Suit yourself."

She put her paws down and stuck her nose into her armpit. Do dogs have armpits?

I broke the silence. "Is he full of shit, or is he just going to leave again in a few weeks when things get difficult?

"I hope not. He's dragged me from one place to another for almost five years. I'm sick of living out of a hotel room. Some places have balconies, but a lot of times he'd lock me up for eight hours at a time. I try to tell him to just let me outside and I'll come back, but he doesn't hear me."

Great. Just fucking great. I get to be interpret the ramblings of an sensitive dog to my clueless father.

"Don't worry, I'm not going to ask you to do anything."

How did she know what I was thinking...oh, forget it. She's inside my head, after all.

"I hope to God we stay here. I really didn't want to leave last time, but he needed me. It shouldn't be a surprise that dogs would rather have a little time outside than being shut in somewhere. Here, it's like fucking paradise. They let me out, I come in."

"I am not talking to a fucking dog,"

"Doesn't hurt to talk to a dog," Martin from maintenance had appeared on my right pulling a floor polisher. "You can tell them anything, they aren't going to talk back or betray your confidence."

Shows how much you know, Mr. Canned asparagus hard boiled eggs cheese and pimentos in a white sauce.

"Think about it. You're sick of the responsibility here. Andy does most of the work here anyway. Your dad has a

lot of talent and needs a place to go. And his dog is sick and tired of road kibble."

"I am not talking to a fucking dog."

The tapping got louder. It was coming from my hand. I looked at it with some surprise and back toward Ruby, but she had disappeared.

November 29

I need to make this quick. Deputy Steel has given me 30 minutes to gather everything that I need for the foreseeable future. This is weird on several levels. He needs to "take me in for questioning" but why would that require an overnight bag? More to the point, if he thinks that I am a criminal how does he know that I'm not destroying evidence right now?

He busted into the office without warning while I had been updating the mailing list, wondering if there was a way to do this on the computer. There were even more questions, he said, but they turned out to be more of the same. Where I was on November 16, and what did I have to do with the destruction of a police car that night. What knowledge do I have of the November 22 disappearance of Lois Hannah, and where I might be hiding her body. I wondered why they would schedule Thanksgiving on the 21st anniversary of the day JFK was shot.

And what did I know about a series of malicious threats sent to all four members of SMUG, designed to discourage the December reunion concert and the further activities of the band itself?

OK, you have me there. I sent out all of the "threats." I know how superstitious Randy can be sometimes, so something unexplainable on black paper was sure to spook him. It had no effect because reuniting SMUG was his life's mission, and he wasn't going to let a few threats get in the way.

As for "threatening" Lois, I answered an ad in the *Village Voice* soliciting odd jobs, and paid them to paper Anita's van.

I didn't count on this. I thought the whole reunion thing was a gimmick that none of us really wanted to do. We were going to get $1,000, which wasn't a heck of a lot to pay four adults to give up a month of their lives so the people they hated in high school could recapture the old days.

I was wrong. Randy was dedicated, and Lois needed the distraction. I needed something to alleviate a crippling boredom and Sparky doesn't really count.

But seriously— I had nothing to do with wrecking Steel's patrol car. I made this comparison a while ago, that I'd rather dig up Mrs. Babian's bones. Pushing a police car over a cliff doesn't make sense on any level, especially for a person whose prime directive is to remain unnoticed.

And Lois. Wherever she is, I have no idea. The notion that I could manipulate her to disappear or do anything to hurt her originate from a better imagination than I'll ever have.

I need to let this unfold. Whatever happens, I will survive. I know that what I did and why, and there is no way that I'll go to jail for this.

They're knocking, gotta go.

Resonance

November 30, 1985

Imagine that, coming back to the Notch one year to the day and the little Cricket is still plugged in, four eyes blinking. When started it chirped, taking me right back to where I was exactly a year and a day ago.

There are some changes. The renovations are almost complete. The glistening structure is visible for hundreds of miles from either direction and the inside of the lodge looks like a restored painting. The café is crowded, and the hotel is full of guests. The family wing was also spruced up, but it's still off limits to the public. My own rooms were polished to a shine, with everything— including the Cricket— put back exactly where it was.

Walter turned the ballroom into a bistro, putting on live shows with a discount room included with each ticket. Come for the concert and you won't have to drive home.

I read this whole disk, 50,000 words worth. It's all about my first 28 years. The way things are now; I could probably write 50,000 more about this past year alone. That's not going to happen, but I may as well try to fill in the blanks.

When Mark Steel bounded into the café, yanked on the handcuffs and frog-walked me to his car he didn't know anything more than the body was found? He assumed that it was Lois, and that I had killed her by sabotaging the cable car. Slam-dunk.

At the Wheeler County Sheriff's office we learned that Lois was not in the car. Rather it was David Steel, our missing mathematician. He had come to the lodge for revenge but saw that the small, sad gathering wasn't worth terrorizing.

He unhooked the cable car and then jumped in, taking it over the crevasse where he cut the line and plunged into a valley of snow.

Dr. Britting, who ruled Wheeler High as head guidance counselor during the blonde fiasco, was now a consulting psychologist for Wheeler County. She explained that David had left a note describing his plan, ending with "Fuck you, Hamster. And fuck you, Mark." She showed us the note, scrawled in a shaky hand accompanied by crude drawings of a squashed rodent and a police car going over a cliff.

Sensitive and socially awkward, our Dave.

"It appears that your brother had neglected to take his medication for the last year," she explained. "He went missing from his important job at the National Bureau of Standards, traveling around the country and ending up here two weeks ago."

At that point I wasn't sure why I was in the room while Dr. Britting made what was essentially a next-of-kin notification. Maybe the old days were returning, where I would be standing in the middle of a room, and nobody knew I was there. Proof of that, I was still wearing handcuffs.

We learned that the medication David was taking allowed him to sublimate his aggressive nature and function in a highly structured, intellectually demanding environment. It didn't disconnect him from reality completely, He was still able to steal a spare key to the cruiser and install his dummy doppelganger to drive it over the cliff.

Sheriff Granger and Mrs. Britting said I was free to go, instructing Steel to drive me back to the Notch. I said no thanks, I'd find my own way. I am not getting into a car with that guy.

For the first time since forever I walked all the way up to the Notch. Snow was everywhere, but they had plowed the shoulder, and it was an easy hike.

Artie was waiting in the café. I sat down at his table, and he didn't say a word. Weird. Artie not jabbering away was as an unusual occurrence as Sparky talking at all.

He told me that Cricket was closing. They'd run out of money after they couldn't accommodate the high percentage of returns. The functioning business was bought by, of all people, Delbert the computer loser, and they were moving it out of Wheeler.

He planned to interview both Artie and Delbert and write a short history that could become a business parable.

Or, I thought, it would bore the asses off everybody and no one would read the whole thing all the way through.

"I can handle the interview," Artie said. "But I can't play host to this vulture. Can you show him around? Or better off, can you put him up here?"

I agreed. When Winterschien's taxi arrived I imagined it would contain a tall skinny guy with a pencil mustache wearing a gray suit and a red tie. Instead, the cab disgorged a short guy, as wide as he was tall, wearing a long ponytail and a long, frizzy beard. He looked familiar, because he had attended the Thanksgiving party in my head.

"You're the bass player," he said before I could introduce myself. "I bought 'Cloud Pictures' when it came out. Great record."

We spent pretty much the next three days together. I drove him around town and to his interviews. In Delbert's office, as the interview was winding down, I asked whether the new company had signed a contract with Intel to supply the 8088 or the 80286 chip, and he responded that the company may dump Intel and go with AMD or another manufacturer as a cost saving measure. I was just curious, but Pete said it was a brilliant question.

We talked, and Pete offered me a job at the magazine, but only if I could start right away.

He told me that the PC business was booming, and the magazine couldn't sell enough advertising. Trouble was, they were selling their advanced knowledge and journalistic analysis, an impossibility with only four writers. Other magazines, better financed, could offer bigger salaries so PC Eye was always the second or third choice.

"It's easier to teach a writer how to be a geek than a geek to be a writer," he said. "You have enough basic knowledge and curiosity, and you act as if you know how to write. As long as you write it in your own voice, not using words that you wouldn't say aloud; you'll do great. We pay $35,000 a year. Except you have to start right away."

"OK," I said. "I'll fly back with you." Not sure if he expected that.

I came in as reviews editor. I managed the products, assigning reviews, and writing a few of my own. I edited the new products/reviews section, which wasn't especially current in a monthly magazine. But, it didn't matter that much since we didn't have a whole lot of competition from the above ground media.

Pete got me an apartment—a "flat"—on Potrero Hill that he had just left when he moved back in with his wife. I'd never lived in a city before. I got a car, a blue Nissan Sentra, but mostly walked or took the bus to work.

There were more people than I'd seen in one place since DC in 1971, and we all know how well that turned out. I found a simple solution, to always know where I was going. Or if I didn't, to look like I knew where I was going. That's the trick of living in a city. After a while, that's all you needed to get around.

Twice a year, Atlanta in the spring and Las Vegas in the fall, the whole staff covered something called COMDEX, a giant trade show where all the new products were shown to an audience of corporations and computer dealers. It was something of a crapshoot. What you saw on the show floor in November could either be on every corporate desk a year later or you would never hear about it again.

I didn't try to figure out what would fly and what would crash. I only reported what people said about their products and then determined if they fulfilled their promise. If something wasn't working correctly I'd point it out, with the caveat that the manufacturer was aware of the glitch and was working toward a solution.

I was a little sponge who knew almost nothing about how computers worked. Someone came in to demo a product, asking if I knew anything about tape backup. I said no, and they spent an hour explaining how it worked and why people should care. I became knowledgeable about tape, and a happy advocate for the company who had provided the education.

The next week someone might come in to pitch a network product and find out that I didn't have the first clue about interoperability. On top of that, the product was a bewildering "networked project manager" that wasn't demonstrated because their tech guy couldn't get our computers to talk to each other.

During that demo a tall guy, the director of marketing, shook my hand enthusiastically but with icy eyes. I knew what he was thinking: What, was I some kind of idiot? I was working at the seventh most important computer magazine and owed it to my readers to be educated. I looked at his card: Willem Wagner, CEO.

Pete came in late, during the demo. Wagner kept talking but paused long enough to pass Pete a card, as did everyone else in the room. At the end of the demo Pete shook hands all around, but it got weird when he came to Wagner.

"It was nice to meet you, Willem," Pete said.

Wagner stiffened and his gray eyes became even frostier.

"That's Villem," making it sound like vellum, or villain," he said sharply, ignoring Pete's outstretched hand.

I wrote a muddled product announcement, borrowing the dead language used in the press release. Wagner called me later saying that I misunderstood the product and should visit their offices in Marin for a full demo. I declined, as I did with all such requests.

Now, when you say the words "network project manager" in any order my eyes roll back into my head and I lose consciousness. It's not like being onstage with SMUG, because I never get to relive fond memories, and people look at me with disdain when I come to. Because what they were saying was really important.

I sat in a lot of meetings. The vendors would make a presentation, showing how their computer would meet a current need or argue that the need wasn't really important. A laptop manufacturer called GRiD had these sleek, black units that were half the size of a regular PC. You could fold the screen down when it wasn't in use, unflattering your desk.

They were working on a battery operated model, requiring heavy cells that only held 30 minutes of power. The PR guy said the machine was targeted toward "business power users," with the average business meeting lasting about half an hour. So the GRiD didn't need a larger battery.

What about the average flight, or even subway ride? That can take longer than a half an hour. I'd see a lot of cool products that could make life more fun, but those aspects were never explored. We are selling to businesses, so our software needs to be boring and our hardware needs to be beige.

All these meetings were the same, so I'd barely pay attention. When they'd finished I'd ask for a press kit and a photo and use that to write the news blurb.

It was more fun at night. Vendors put on parties to outdo each other. The bottom line is that journalists could eat like a pig and drink like a fish, only spending about $4 in a week's time. In Atlanta one vendor rented out the Fox Theater for a Four Tops show. I got really drunk and ended up dancing in the orchestra pit while Tops lead singer Levi Stubbs bent down and gave everyone a high-five. Our hands met the same time as our eyes, with his saying something like "neither of us has any business being here."

In Las Vegas last week the magazine took everyone to see Siegfried and Roy at the Frontier. There was a long chorus line of women, wearing ornate red costumes that gave off a dazzling glare. I watched them for several minutes before realizing that their bodies were fully covered while their breasts were exposed.

The next night we went to a reception for an operating environment called Microsoft Windows. It was a ridiculous program, it sat between the operating system and the applications, imposing a graphical interface with pull down menus. Except Windows slowed down the hardware, and there was no software that used the interface.

After the reception six of piled into my rental car and each threw a copy of Windows in the trunk. After the next party, we noticed that the trunk was jimmied open. The thieves hadn't bothered to steal the so-called fancy new software program but had made off with five promotional umbrellas and several t-shirts. In a review, I suggested that Windows would never succeed until people thought that it was worth stealing.

One year ago the Notch was getting too crowded for me, I just wanted to get away from all the people who were sucking me dry. In San Francisco I just do my job and no one asks for anything extra. So I'm in the Notch for a visit, but I'm going to live in San Francisco for a while. I came for a short visit thinking it would be exhilarating, instead the Notch now feels claustrophobic.

When I lived here people would talk about the world outside, but I had no interest. Everything I needed was here. I didn't have to work. I could do whatever I wanted. Play at being a hotel manager. Play music. Write. Go on hikes. Except it got to the point where I didn't want to do any of that either.

I wake up in San Francisco every day, ready to explore every corner of the city. I walk forever, landing in tattered bookstores and cheap bars. I understand there is a whole different world across the Bay in Berkeley or north to Marin, but I'll get there whenever I'm ready.

I couldn't move back here and have it be the same, as Walter has taken over management of the Notch. In his past stretch as manager he was kind of a slug, giving orders to the staff if something needs to be done or fixed. I followed that tradition, acting a bit like a pampered prince.

I got to meet Denise, my mother, when she spoke at a conference in town. As an FCC commissioner she was charged with regulating radio and TV, but this was due to expand when people started using computers to connect to news sources. It is important to lay the groundwork for this eventuality, she said, although she was the only one on the five-member commission who believed this.

We had dinner afterwards, and she came over to the flat for a drink. It was uncomfortable for a little while. It turned out that she felt guilty that she didn't feel worse about "abandoning" me, and I wondered if there were something missing in me because I didn't hold a grudge. Once we got that out of the way we had long talks about computers, music and the Notch.

She said that Mrs. Babian watched over me when I was a kid, sending Denise regular dispatches about my successes and drawbacks. She'd heard about my unfortunate nickname and was gleeful when David Steel got his comeuppance.

I wasn't sure what she meant.

"My mother was a talented sorceress," she said. "I saw her turn people into goats many times. They'd be on the trail, and she'd do her magic, they'd walk up the hill and she'd change them back again. They'd regain their own physical form 200 yards up the mountain and have no recollection how they got there.

"You could always tell which goats used to be people, because they had only a single antler."

You lost me, Mom.

She also had her own interpretation of Steel's suicide. It had less to do with the medication than a strong residual memory of becoming a goat for two weeks. As a wild animal he was free to stick his horn into other beings, and he missed the feeling. When he told the therapist about becoming a goat she increased the medication to near catatonia. At that time, the only thing he could do was math.

This was a little startling, up to that point she had made a lot of sense.

She said she wanted to write a book about how personal computers will change how people communicate and receive information, asking whether I'd be interested in co-authoring the project. Goats notwithstanding, I said it was a great idea and we should work on an outline. I thought it would be one of those grand ideas that fall through the cracks, but she sent me an outline which I rewrote into a book proposal.

At COMDEX, I met with a publisher who approved the concept and promised to send me a contract. We want to write this quickly since tech progress is a bit of a moving target.

Once David Steel's body had been recovered people began wondering where Lois went. It was assumed that she had died in an accident, leaving several people to continue her ideas. The *Anita: Hand* album was finished and was rush-released to capitalize on her disappearance.

The rest of the band just waited for Lois to assume the Anita mantle, but she stayed missing. The completed album included Lois' vocals, but the band practiced live versions with a replacement. They didn't have to change anything else, as the cover pictures of the band were fuzzy and could have been anybody.

The best part of this was the replacement vocalist's given name was Anita. The rest of the band saw this as a good sign, until it turned out that the replacement Anita was far less collaborative and easygoing than Lois.

Randy lost all the color in his face and the spring in his step when Lois disappeared. We tried a rehearsal to move our minds beyond the tragedy but didn't connect with each other at all.

I couldn't wait to tell him about Steel, that Lois was not in the cable car which meant she was elsewhere. I called his work and then his house. His boss said that he hadn't shown up in two days, and there was no answer at home.

Anita: Hand did well enough, boosted by the quality of the music and the quasi-psychedelic cover. Music has become less exciting than any other recent period I can remember, and this record looked, sounded and felt like nothing else now available.

Except for another album that came out a month later, titled *SMUG: Resonance.* This was a tape of SMUG's last show edited down to a double album while including most of Randy's wild soloing. "Spirit in the Sky," which was cut from *Anita: Hand*, took up an entire side. Its cover was a send-up of the Anita album, the typestyle and title location were in the exact same spot and the cover image was the negative reinterpretation of the cover.

Both records were released in the spring. *SMUG: Resonance* ended up outselling *Anita: Hand*, which was good news for me because I was getting royalties. There were a few articles over the summer about Lois' disappearance, and the notion that it was a big publicity stunt. One of her old band members was sure that she would engineer her own reappearance at the opportune time.

I wasn't convinced. I didn't think she was dead, but she didn't strike me as the type to set up a resurrection drama. Many musicians hit it big in their early 20s. Lois would turn 29 during the planned Anita tour. She had worked hard over the past few years in anonymity, and was drawing on this relative maturity to better prepare her for any media attention.

"At first I thought you were being a prima donna, by saying you didn't want to play in public," she said. "But I really get it now. Many musicians thrive on the connection with the audience, in sort of an energy cycle. I think the music is purest when there is no psychic interference from an audience, where you can just play what's in your heart without having to care about how it sounds to anybody else."

Her turnaround was a surprise, because she had always been the band member most frustrated by my stage fright quirk. We actually got into an argument about it once, during SMUG's first go-round.

"There is a difference between a quirk and a flaw," she said. "A quirk is a behavioral oddity, mildly annoying yet ultimately amusing. A flaw is something that keeps you from greatness or even half-greatness, and hinders those around you."

She drove her point home, saying that I really didn't have quirks. All my eccentricities were flaws.

Today, she is most likely to call my stage phobia an asset that she wouldn't mind sharing. She was driven to perform, share her art, be recognized as a serious creator.

Last year, she only reached a state of calm while we were playing. As soon as we stopped her shoulders slumped and she ran into the lobby to call her manager about an ancillary issue that had nothing at all to do with the music. She'd return, and it would take her one full song to pick up the groove again. It wouldn't be noticeable to anyone outside the band, as the three of us were playing in and out of each others' heads.

In late October, I was walking in North Beach, noting that it was nearly a year since Lois disappeared, wondering if any of the music papers would commemorate that anniversary. I guessed not, as the music press had forgotten about Lois and were in a lather about Kate Bush. There was only room for one wildly eccentric female singer at a time.

I sat on a park bench, watching the buskers play to the passers by. There were three; a woman and a much taller man playing guitars and someone of uncertain gender on finger cymbals and bells. They were wearing saffron robes that offset their shaved heads.

When I sat down they were playing a hypnotic chant. Even though there were only three of them each repetition changed and seemed to add something new. It reminded me of SMUG, and I became a little sad about the lost opportunity. I know I wanted to quit the band, but if it happened today I would have made it happen.

They finished the chant, leading directly to a 4/4 pattern on the cymbals and bells. A chugging "A" riff followed, again building with each measure. They began singing in high thin voices, sounding much like the tiny women in "Mothra vs. Godzilla" crossed with Alvin and the Chipmunks.

"When I die and they lay me to rest, gonna go to the place that's the best. When they lay me down to die I'm going up to the spirit in the sky."

Not as much power as SMUG's version, or even Anita's, but it was still catchy and reminded me of the past. Music is a wonderful uniter, as one song can have many versions and still retain its meaning. The spiritual subject added to the ethereal feeling.

They extended the song to nearly 15 minutes, which didn't seem repetitive because the people walking by never heard more than a stanza or two. They finished and began packing up their gear.

I walked up to the woman, whom I now recognized as Lois.

"That might be the best version of that song I'd ever heard."

I expected she might drop her guitar, go "holy shit!!" and give me a huge hug. Instead, she gave me one of her enigmatic little smiles. Randy turned around and gave a little start, but acted that it was completely natural to meet someone who thought he might be dead in a San Francisco park.

"Oh, hey," he said. "Want to get a beer?" Not waiting for an answer he said they had to change first and asked me to watch their stuff.

There was a public toilet nearby. They emerged after five minutes wearing street clothes and knit caps, carrying their robes in a shoulder bag. The three of us headed into the nearest bar.

"What about sh—him?" I asked, nodding toward the cymbal player.

"Oh, he's just going back to the temple," Randy said. "He used to drum in a band but likes to get away from the temple a few times a week."

"Too bad you couldn't get Sparky," I said.

"Oh no," Lois said. "That is Sparky."

Of course it is.

We sat down wordlessly. I broke the silence, telling them how I'd met Pete when he came to Wheeler to do the post mortem on Cricket Computer, and he talked me into a job. Filling the space, I marveled about how an irritable hermit had become one of the top 200 computer journalists in San Francisco in ten short months.

"What about you guys?" They can't jerk me around like this.

We got another round as Randy began the tale. On Thanksgiving Eve last year they had decided to pull the plug on SMUG and give Anita-the-band a natural end.

"I had enough of that life," Lois said. "There was too much pressure around Anita, and the fun part was over. SMUG was a nice respite, but if we took it any further it would be the same insane game."

She found she loved playing with Randy and wanted to fold him into Anita-the-band. That idea was shut down unmercifully, and Lois was told to get her ass back to New York immediately.

They hatched the plan where Lois would pretend to disappear and drive to Colorado Springs where she'd hook up with Randy. They'd figure out next steps from there, how to play music without playing the fame game.

They didn't count on David Steel's little stunt, and were surprised to hear about the missing cable car and the assumption that I was a murderer.

"That was unfortunate," she said. "I would have come back and said I wasn't dead if it went on too long. Steel did us a favor, providing a distraction so I could slip out of town."

As part of the plan Lois had pulled out $15,000 from her account, figuring that would last a while. Her personal manager, who was also her sister, was in on the scam. Linda was receiving all the new royalties and would send them along when needed.

"We can pretend to be Hare Krishna street musicians forever," she said. "But it's already getting a little old. So we'll probably go to Portland and Seattle and perform as a folk duo. We'll keep shaving our heads, because when you do that no one really sees your face."

I gave them my PC Eye card, writing my home number on the back.

"Send me a postcard or something and let me know where you are," I said. "I've been up to Seattle a few times and we can go see a show or something."

They got up and we all hugged. Outside we hugged again. Randy walked halfway down the block, and then turned back. He handed me a cassette.

"Often times, when we play our sacred chants there is resonance," he said. "We got it on tape."

Resonance

Paul Trout is a retired veteran of the personal technology industry. He lives in the Pacific Northwest where he plays bass for a Neil Young tribute band. For more information contact pt.resonance@gmail.com.

Made in the USA
Columbia, SC
25 April 2018